"We might find another connection between the victims if we dig deep enough," Chloe said.

She turned to face him, took a chance. "But I'd guess, after looking at the evidence so far, that the real target of all that pent-up rage was you."

Jake's hands fisted, his only show of temper. Though his vivid blue eyes burned with anger, he kept his voice low, controlled. "Why?"

She didn't touch him, just watched. "Why what, Pastor?"

"Why kill her? Why wouldn't he come after me instead?"

"Because he wanted you to hurt worse than you have ever hurt in your life. And the numbers on the wall indicate that he'll keep killing. Unless I'm way off base...he isn't done torturing you yet."

Books by Stephanie Newton

Love Inspired Suspense

*Perfect Target
*Moving Target
*Smoke Screen

*Emerald Coast 911

STEPHANIE NEWTON

penned her first suspense story—complete with illustrations—at the age of twelve, but didn't write seriously until her youngest child was in first grade. She lives in northwest Florida, where she gains inspiration from the sugar-white sand, aqua blue-green water of the Gulf of Mexico, and the many unusual and interesting things you see when you live on the beach. You can find her most often enjoying the water with her family, or at their church, where her husband is the pastor. Visit Stephanie at her Web site, www.stephanienewton.net or send an e-mail to newtonwriter@gmail.com.

SMOKE SCREEN

STEPHANIE NEWTON

Steeple Hill®

Published by Steeple Hill Books™

STEEPLE HILL BOOKS

Steeple
Hill®

Recycling programs
for this product may
not exist in your area.

ISBN-13: 978-0-373-44378-9

SMOKE SCREEN

www.SteepleHill.com

Printed in U.S.A.

Where can I go from Your Spirit?
Where can I flee from Your presence?
If I go up to the heavens, You are there;
if I make my bed in the depths, You are there.
If I rise on the wings of the dawn,
if I settle on the far side of the sea,
Even there Your hand will guide me,
Your right hand will hold me fast.
—*Psalms* 139:7–10

Many, many thanks are due to all those who contributed to making this book a reality.

For the technical info, I have to give credit to those way smarter than I am for so much that I didn't know. Any mistakes…well, those I'll take full credit for.

So, *gracias, merci, xie xie, grazie,* thank you, thank you, thank you…

First, to my family, for being so understanding, and (almost) always supportive of having pizza just one more time.

To my awesome editor, Melissa Endlich, and my amazing agent, Barbara Collins Rosenberg—it's my great honor to be working with you.

To my writing "support group," Brenda Minton, Catherine Mann and Holly La Pat—for the brainstorming, coffee breaks, late-night critiques and super-fast reads, especially when you are so busy with your own work.

To Brian Stampfl, of CSI Seattle—for answering my questions and keeping me from making dumb mistakes.

To Joe and Susie Endry—for your generosity. I wouldn't have made my deadline without you!

Finally, to Joe Reeder, firefighter-EMT with Bay County Fire-Rescue—for the help, for letting your wife befriend the new pastor's wife, for what you do every day. I'm truly grateful.

ONE

"Units requested for structure fire at 1215 Conch Drive. Flames visible." Jake Rollins tossed the red bubble light onto the dash of his 4Runner as the scanner continued its commentary from the floorboard. He was going to miss his meeting.

The calls sometimes came in the middle of the night. Fire didn't have an alarm clock and accidents didn't have a time schedule. Little children didn't get lost—and found—according to what was convenient for emergency personnel.

"Units responding."

Jake shifted gears, preacher to firefighter. He might not be a smoke-eater anymore, but he still fought fires his own way, fighting the damage they did—to their victims and to the people who walked fearlessly into them—every day. Fire had almost destroyed him.

It was only the grace of God that had saved him, only God that could have brought him back from the pit he'd been in when he'd discovered he couldn't be a firefighter anymore. God had given him a new purpose, serving others in a way that he hadn't been able to before—and working for the department in a way that would never have been cool to him before—as Sea Breeze, Florida's, first fire department chaplain.

He leaned over to turn the scanner up, listening for details. Emergency vehicles and beach traffic didn't mix well. A horn blared as he shot into an opening in the next lane.

Jake whipped into the neighborhood, pulling to a stop. A smear of charcoal-gray smoke in the sky told him he was in the right place without him even checking the address. Police had closed off the perimeter, but the turnout gear that he was required to wear on scene eased the way. The crew from his old station house was on duty. Two firefighters trained spray from the heavy hose onto the burning structure and Captain Caruso wore a path in the lawn, barking orders into his walkie-talkie.

Tension tightened Jake's shoulders. When things went well at a job, the men who fought the fires cracked jokes to handle the stresses of a high-pressure job. That was a good day.

When they didn't get to a scene in time—when there was a victim, or when the structure was too compromised to stay inside and fight—that was a bad day. Two of his friends stumbled through the smoke pouring out the open front door. As they got closer to the captain, firefighter Todd Blankenship shook his head. Not a good day.

The muscles in Jake's arms twitched. He wanted to be in there—every fire, every time. He'd been trained for this, born for this, but his injury limited his motion and effectively ended his career with the fire department. It didn't end his desire to be in the middle of the action, to make up somehow for failing to do his job when it mattered most.

Jake stepped up beside the captain as Todd pushed his faceplate back. "We were too late."

"You got a name, Cap?" Jake checked out the structure. It barely looked like a house anymore. Smoke poured from every crevice, hot orange flames licking at the roofline.

The captain rifled through a clipboard of papers. "Sharon Hardin."

Fire punched through the roof as recognition punched Jake in the gut. He knew Sharon. She went to his church, had been coordinating a mission trip. They'd been working closely together to organize the overseas trip, meeting regularly to hammer out the details.

He'd taken her for coffee three days ago.

Flames shot into the sky with crackling laughter. The captain rubbed the back of his hand across his mouth. "Clark and Hughes still in there?"

"Yes, sir." Blankenship pushed a weary hand through sweaty hair.

"Team four, get out now. Get out now."

The walkie-talkie crackled. "Two minutes, sir."

"*Now,* Hughes."

"Copy that."

Jake could hear the dejection in Lara Hughes's voice. She wouldn't want to talk, but she would need to, later.

They all would, but for now, they needed to get out of that structure while they still had time.

Thirty seconds stretched as, outside, firefighters cooled the blaze with a powerful stream of water. They waited for the two-person team to exit the building. The seconds ticked by until finally, head down, Hughes came out full speed. Smoke billowed around Matt Clark as he followed her out. He thrust his helmet back, his grimy, sooty face bleak.

The squad's captain waited for him to get close. "What's the word, Clark?"

"She was already dead when we went in." Clark unbuckled his gear. "The inspectors are gonna have a ton of evidence to collect on this one. Something weird went down in there."

The captain stared into the smoke as if he could figure out the answers just from studying it. Sometimes it seemed to Jake that he could.

A shout came from the other side of the building. Captain Caruso strode toward it, leaving Jake with Lara Hughes. His throat burned. The smoke, maybe. Maybe just too many remembered emotions crowding in where they didn't belong. Not on the job—even when, maybe especially when, a friend had died in that house.

Lara pulled her helmet off, revealing a sweaty blond ponytail. Jake squeezed her shoulder. "You okay?"

"Yeah. It was a tough one, finding her like that. I thought maybe we'd gotten here in time when the cops told us that was her car out front. But she didn't have a chance." Lara Hughes kicked at the grass, dry beneath their feet.

"There's not anyone here who would fight harder for a victim than you."

Lara Hughes, who would take on any man out here in a shoving match, grabbed Jake in a tight hug. "I know that. But thanks."

With the fire now out, she slammed her helmet back on her head and went into the building to begin the cleanup. Jake stared after her, his gut aching for the men and women of his old crew who were dealing with a tough loss today. For himself, he couldn't begin to process it.

Matt Clark stuck his head out the front door of the building. "Jake, come in here. Cap says you need to see this."

He pushed through the ruined front door. The still-smoking building cracked and hissed. Water dripped from every surface. The stench of soggy, burned fabric and carpet, while familiar, still overwhelmed him.

The firefighters, his friends, wouldn't meet his eyes. Something was wrong. More wrong than a woman dying in a fire. Dread and anxiety knotted inside him as he looked from face to face.

He angled past them farther into the room, where he could see the evidence that this fire probably didn't start by accident. What looked like multiple points of origin made uneven burn patterns on the walls.

"She's in here." Captain Caruso poked his head out from the bedroom door. "Don't touch anything."

Jake stepped into the room and nearly grabbed for the door frame before he caught himself. He'd walked into a nightmare—one he didn't have nightly any-more, but still often enough to make his stomach rebel at the sight.

The captain reached for his shoulder. "Jake, take it easy."

Clad in a girlish white dress, Sharon had been placed on the bed, her arms crossed at the waist. On her left hand was a slim embossed gold ring that Jake would bet didn't belong to her. He knew without looking what would be on the night table. And when he glanced over, he saw he was right—a silver cross and a tiny glass figurine of a dancing girl. Wilted flowers.

"Why didn't this burn?" His voice sounded strangled, even to himself.

"Best I can figure, the arsonist sprayed some kind of fire retardant on it. There's an odor you can just get a whiff of. We'll know more after the evidence is tested." Matt Clark had been his best friend while he served the fire department. He punched Jake in the shoulder. "Hey, you okay?"

"We need to preserve the scene." The captain looked up from his clipboard. "Someone call Cruse Conyers at the SBPD and get the crime-scene unit here."

"I'll try to find out who her next of kin is." How strange that Jake could know the right thing to say.

Every piece of the carefully set scene matched his last fire. The fire that had killed his fiancée, Julie. The dress, the flowers that maybe she bought herself but no one could remember seeing her buy. Even the figurine that he knew didn't belong to her but couldn't be proven.

Everyone in his crew knew that fire had been set but no one had ever been able to establish it wasn't accidental.

"Jake?" Matt Clark stepped up beside him, his turnout gear rustling in the strangely quiet house, the dripping water the only other sound. "What do you make of that?"

The wall above the bed hadn't burned. It didn't look damaged from the fire at all. But in the center of the wall, someone had spray-painted a big number two and circled it.

"I think he's telling us there will be more." The captain resettled his helmet on his head. He looked directly at Jake. "And it implies there was a number one."

Jake didn't have to ask who the number one was. He knew. "Julie."

Everyone had assumed that her killer had been passing through. That she'd been a random target, chosen while she was jogging down the beach, or followed home from the grocery store. And though they assumed he had killed before because he was too organized, they figured he'd moved on, that he wouldn't be back here in this small Florida town where everyone knew everyone else.

The captain broke the silence. "Hughes, get the cops on the horn, and tell everyone to keep a lid on it."

The last thing the captain would want was a leak that they had a serial arsonist, much less a serial killer around town. The panic that would ensue would be difficult if not impossible to control.

As Jake studied the number two on the wall, the paint

underneath it began to bubble. The room filled with a crackling noise, like the sound of Rice Krispies in milk. "Captain, rekindle."

Instantly the room erupted in motion, the captain yelling into his walkie-talkie. "Get a hose in here."

As Matt Clark punched a fist-sized hole in the wall waist high, the captain pushed at the head of the bed. "Rollins, help me get the bed out of the way. We need to preserve as much of this as we can."

Jake hauled the bed across the room as the captain pushed from the other side. His damaged back protested with a stab of pain. Hughes tossed him a tarp.

He settled it over the top of the bed in an effort to preserve the scene for the arson investigators and crime-scene detectives. Every piece of evidence counted. Fighting the fire wasn't his responsibility anymore, but taking care of the victims was, even if this victim— Sharon—would never know.

Smoke filled the room again as the firefighters crowded into the small space, suppressing the fire that had hidden in the walls, sneaky little thief that it was. The old house groaned and dripped, the whole thing a backdrop for a horrible crime.

Who would do such a twisted thing to Sharon? Could Julie's killer have come back to strike again three years later? It didn't make sense. Why now? Why Sharon? He'd been spending a good bit of time with her because of the upcoming mission trip.

He didn't like the train of thought his mind was taking. He knew the time spent with Sharon had just been coffee and they'd only talked about church business, but did the killer? Because the only link he could think of between Sharon Hardin and his fiancée…was him.

Two days later, Supervisory Special Agent Chloe Davis rolled into a town she'd never expected to see again once she'd transferred to the FBI's Serial Crimes Unit. Sea Breeze, Florida, was a picturesque beachside village with just the right mix of kitsch and charm. It made her palms itch.

Give her the big city any day. The crowds, the noise, the anonymity. She'd spent too much time undercover to want it—need it—any other way.

She pulled into the parking lot at the police station, a tall, nondescript gray building. Leaning on the window of a red Toyota 4Runner was an old friend. She and Gabe Sloan had worked a case together, though he hadn't known that for most of it. She'd been undercover trying to expose a drug-smuggling ring. His fiancée, Sailor, had been one of her suspects. And when someone tried to kill Sailor, Chloe'd been one of *his*.

When she slammed the door of her Honda Accord, he turned around. After a moment's scrutiny a wide smile split his face. "Well, if it isn't our teenage urchin. Not looking so waiflike anymore."

She glanced down at her slim black pants and suit jacket, her gold badge attached at the hip. "No, full professional form today. Not as much fun as playing a hooker or impersonating a high-priced lawyer, but not as dangerous—most days. My insurance company is happy at least."

As she spoke, she took note of the other man. Early to mid-thirties, nice-looking, hot and sweaty, a little rough around the edges, maybe. His face was dirty, his blue eyes red-rimmed. Still, some indefinable quality made her want to step closer, see what was behind those eyes.

He pushed the door to his truck open and she automatically shifted her stance to a defensive one. Gabe noticed, but only smiled as the guy's feet hit the pavement. And as they did, she saw why the dude's eyes were red-rimmed. He was a firefighter. He'd taken off his turnout coat, but he still wore the heavy Nomex pants and boots.

"Supervisory Special Agent Chloe Davis, meet my friend Jake Rollins. Forgive his appearance, Chloe, he's been busy inhaling a little smoke today."

Jake's eyes darted to meet Gabe's. "Special Agent…? She's with the FBI? So, she's here…"

"Chloe's recently been assigned to the Serial Crimes Unit. She's here as a special favor to me. Sharon's death two days ago brought a whole new aspect to this case that we hadn't expected. Until we figure out the nature of the criminal we're dealing with, we can follow the physical evidence, but we have precious little to go on. That's what Chloe's here for."

"But…" Whatever he'd been about to say, he swallowed it back, nodding instead, before turning to his truck. "I'd better get to work."

"Hey, Rollins. When I was at the scene today, you were holding a mother's hand. Did they find the kid?"

"A five-year-old girl." Sea-blue eyes met Chloe's and held. "They found her under the bed, probably the best air in the house. She's going to be okay."

"Great news." Gabe smacked his hands together, drawing Jake's attention.

The firefighter looked back at Gabe. "Yeah, it was nice meeting you, Chloe. Be seeing you." He slid into his truck and slammed the door.

Chloe shifted her gaze from the disappearing 4Runner back to Gabe. "What's his connection to the case?"

"His fiancée was the first victim."

"Oh." She frowned.

"It's not like that. He was on duty when the crime happened and nearly died trying to get her out of the fire. He was in the hospital for weeks. He couldn't regain full function. He had to quit fighting fires."

"And yet, the uniform?"

"Oh, Jake's not a firefighter. He's the chaplain."

Oh, no. What was that she'd said about being a hooker? "He's a…"

Gabe grinned. "Yeah, honey. That guy you were just making eyes at is my pastor."

"I was not making eyes at anyone." Much less a pastor.

Gabe held the door open for her. She paused, then walked through. None of her coworkers at Quantico would dare hold the door open for her, but then, she wasn't at Quantico. She was in the deep South, where manners were as ingrained as the ability to spot a fake a mile away, whether it was fake blonde, fake silver or fake motives.

She punched the button for the elevator. "I've read the background. I know about the original case, the new victim and the number two on the wall. But why would you call me for assistance now? It's early."

Gabe stepped onto the elevator, turned back to her. "Because we don't think he's going to stop."

Three hours later, steeped in the facts of the case, Chloe drove down the coastal highway, the turquoise waters of the Gulf of Mexico deepening to emerald-green as the sun lowered. She'd gotten Jake Rollins's address from the file. It was now clear why Gabe had called in that favor she owed him. This case had layers and she had questions. Questions only Jake could answer.

The pastor of the Community Fellowship Church lived in a tiny condo across from the waterfront. From the Toyota in the driveway, she figured he was home. She walked to the door, cursing her redheaded fair skin that heated as she remembered her earlier remarks about her undercover work posing as a prostitute.

Jake Rollins opened the door, his dark hair damp and curling over the collar of a ragged well-worn polo. He didn't smile. "Special Agent Davis."

"Chloe. I have some questions."

He opened the door wider. "I have coffee on."

She walked into his condo, looking around at the clearly masculine space. The newspaper was spread on the coffee table and mugs littered the end tables, but chocolate-brown walls made it feel cozy rather than cluttered.

She stopped when she reached the breakfast nook. A file box was open on the oak table. Photos of a burned-out building were scattered on the surface, along with photocopies of evidence logs and reports. She wheeled to face him. "Where did you get these?"

"I was off my feet for months after the accident. It haunted me—the scene, what happened and who could have done it." Jake's expression breathed misery. "Why I couldn't stop it. I called the police and the fire department every day asking questions, begging them to tell me what they knew. Finally, my friends there figured that maybe it would be better if I had what they had. They made me copies. After a while, I stopped asking questions."

He walked to the window looking over his tiny backyard. "Last year I packed Julie's things in the box with the evidence file and put it in the top of my closet. I didn't think I would ever look in that box again."

She picked up a photograph of a beautiful young brunette, laughing into the camera. "She doesn't look like our current victim."

"No." He turned back to study the picture, his eyes narrowing in concentration as he considered her question.

Chloe didn't know why she felt such compassion for this man. She came in contact with the families of murder victims every day. Maybe it was the loss of a career he loved and his determination to continue serving those who suffered, even if he didn't do it in the same way. Maybe she was just a sucker for big blue eyes and a five-o'clock shadow. "Can you walk me through it? Your relationship…the crime?"

His jaw bunched. "How does this help find a killer?"

"To understand a killer, I have to know the victims." She walked to the coffeepot in his granite-and-stainless-steel kitchen. "Do you mind?"

"Please, make yourself at home."

She poured herself a cup and settled on the couch, the leather creaking as she sat.

His brows drew together. Talking about her had to be hard for him. It had been a loss that he probably still felt every day, if he was human. This new crime would only make that old wound raw and new again.

"Where's your team? I thought the FBI always worked in teams."

"We're in between cases and I'm checking into this as a favor to Gabe." She sipped the strong black brew. "Don't worry. I work very well alone."

"Now why doesn't that surprise me?" He kept his features blank as he sat on the opposite end of the couch from her.

She shot him a look. "If I decide the case warrants the full team, I'll ask for them. Otherwise, their time is better utilized on other projects."

He gestured to the box on the table. "What do you want to know?"

Chloe picked up the crime-scene photographs, forcing herself to look at them as a puzzle to be deciphered, something starting to come more easily to her with practice. She'd been in the Serial Crimes Unit for nine months. Seeing what one human would choose to do to another... At first, she hadn't slept. Slowly, she began to realize that the scenes she studied were someone else's story, not her own. She was a bystander. An objective witness, not a participant.

Her story involved taking down the criminals that committed the crimes. Making sure that they didn't happen to another innocent victim. And she was good at it. "I looked at these at the police station. This is only a preliminary finding, but I'd say that this crime wasn't one of opportunity. It took time to stage, time to set up. He didn't choose her at random. He chose her for a purpose."

The pastor's knee began to bounce, but he stayed on the sofa beside her.

"We might find another connection between the victims if we dig deep enough." She turned to face him, took a chance. "But I'd guess, after looking at these, that the real target of all that pent-up rage was you."

Jake Rollins's hands fisted, his only show of temper. Though his vivid blue eyes burned with anger, he kept his voice low, controlled. "Why?"

She didn't touch him, just watched. "Why what, Pastor?"

"Why kill her? Why wouldn't he come after me instead?"

"Because he wanted you to hurt worse than you have ever hurt in your life. And the numbers on the wall indicate that he'll keep killing. He isn't done torturing you yet."

TWO

Jake opened the door to the church office, silencing the security alarm before it could announce his presence to the neighborhood. Today was Saturday, so the office would be quiet, and hopefully he would have a couple of hours before his phone started ringing again.

Within minutes, he had his favorite blend of coffee brewing and his mail in his hand. His normal routine—yet he felt anything but normal. He let the mail scatter to the counter. How could he do ordinary things, when his world had been turned upside down again? The guilt that he'd struggled to put behind him had come flooding back with Sharon Hardin's death.

He hadn't been there for Julie, not the one time it really counted. And now, he'd let down another woman he cared about, even if Sharon had just been a friend. God helped. Of course Jake knew that. He wouldn't have survived after the accident without God's leading. Without God's presence.

He could get through this, too—if he didn't try to do it alone.

He poured a cup of coffee and gathered his mail again, thinking he didn't really need some madman torturing him. He was doing a pretty good job of that himself. And maybe that was the point.

A soft tapping sounded behind him. "Is that fresh coffee I smell?"

Jake smiled at Gabe and gestured at the coffeepot. "Help yourself. As if your wife doesn't make the best in town."

"She's been a little busy lately getting ready for the baby, and trying to find just the right combination of artists to show in the gallery section of the shop has been harder than she thought."

Jake tossed his mail on his desk and plopped into his desk chair. "So is this a friendly visit or professional?"

"A little bit of both. We're pals, right?" Gabe took a swig from his coffee mug.

"Of course we are." Jake watched Gabe pace the room, pretending to study the various trinkets from mission trips around the world. Africa, Honduras, Brazil.

The quiet stretched as the big cop stopped to tap a finger down the books on the bookshelf before dusting it off on his jeans. "It's a lot to handle, finding out that Julie might not have been a random pick by that killer. And Sharon…it would be a lot for anyone to handle."

"Sailor made you check on me, didn't she?"

Gabe's eyes slid away. "That obvious, huh?"

"Yeah. It's still nice to have friends who care. I'm fine. But, Gabe, we have to catch this guy."

"We will. So how did it go with Chloe yesterday?"

He looked into his mug, a smile tugging at his lips. She'd poured herself another cup of coffee last night before she'd even gotten through the photos. "It went okay. It's hard for me to be objective. She wanted to dig into the past with Julie. I did some research after she left. Victimology, I think they call it."

"Studying the victims in a criminal investigation sometimes provides clues to why they were chosen, why that person fulfilled the fantasy of the offender. If we can figure out how the perpetrator chose his victim, that information can sometimes lead to the next one before it's too late. It's not an exact science." Gabe sat in the chair across from the desk and leaned forward toward Jake. "It's more than we had, though."

Jake stabbed a hand through his hair, a nervous habit that had driven his grandmother crazy. "Knowing why she's poking into my past doesn't make it any less painful. Or weird."

"No, probably not. And Chloe can be intense. It makes her good at her job, but a little hard to live with. She was unbelievable last year, though. I never would've guessed she was FBI. I was convinced she was out to rob Sailor blind."

"She's going to be asking more questions today."

"Then I should let you enjoy whatever quiet time you have left." Gabe got to his feet. As he passed Jake's desk, he pointed to a red tin. "Women still baking you cookies all the time?"

Jake grinned. "I should never have mentioned in that

sermon that chocolate chip–walnut were my favorite."
He opened the lid. "Have one?"

"Are you kidding me? I've put on five pounds of
pregnancy weight already and Sailor's only four months
along. The bad thing is that Sailor will lose all that she
gains and I won't. In fact, I think I'm gonna go for a run.
In a few months when the baby comes, I won't have
time to exercise."

As Gabe left, Jake looked into the tin of cookies. He
loved cookies any time of day, but he didn't even feel
like eating them. He tossed the lid onto the desk. The
unanswered questions churned in his gut. Maybe if he
could look at the time spent with Chloe as doing something, instead of just sitting around waiting for something to happen, it would help.

The sound of high heels on the tile floor of the church
alerted him to the presence of someone else in the
building. When Chloe poked her head around the door
to his office, he wasn't surprised.

She had on another trim suit—this one charcoal-
gray—and about three-inch heels, probably designed to
make her look older and taller.

"Do you realize that there are signs leading anyone
who wants *directly* to you? Church Office, Pastor's
Study. The front door was unlocked and as far as I can
tell, you are the only person in the building. Does that
happen a lot?"

Jake leaned his desk chair back and crossed his arms.
"Good morning, Special Agent Davis."

Chloe whirled to face him, deep auburn hair swinging around her shoulders, a scowl on her face. "What?"

"It's a customary greeting for early in the day. If you'd like coffee, there's a fresh pot in the conference room across the hall. Please, make yourself at home." He tilted a smile at her.

A tint of pink shaded her cheeks, but she just shrugged. "Lack of security tends to put me on edge."

"It's a church."

"What does that have to do with anything?"

"People having access to it and finding their way around is kind of the point." He drained his cup and pushed to his feet.

"Where are you going?"

He tilted the mug at her. "My cup's empty."

She followed him into the conference room. "I know the temptation is to go about your life like everything is normal. It's natural that you want to make things the way they were before."

He put the coffeepot back on the burner as gently as he could master and rested his palms flat on the counter. "Don't you think I know things aren't normal, Chloe?"

"I'm sure you do, but…" She stopped and laid her hand on his. "Look, I'm sorry, Jake. I know this can't be easy for you."

He looked at their hands, his brown and scarred, hers small and fair. He was surprised at how delicate hers was, considering she seemed so capable, somehow larger than life, that irrepressible energy almost shimmering beneath the surface.

He reached for another mug, pulling his hand out from hers. "Coffee?"

"Sure, because I could really use the caffeine."

"You made a joke."

She took the coffee from him. "I have been known to. Just don't get used to it."

"Come on. I'll show you around and you can ask me anything you want."

Her eyes, dark chocolate brown, softened. "Believe it or not, I do understand being thrown by your circumstances into a new situation and wishing like anything you could go back to yesterday. You try as hard as you can to pretend that you aren't hurting…and to some extent you should do that. The last thing you want is for the killer to think he has power over you. That's what he wants." She paused. "But in order to stay safe, you may have to admit that you need help. That things are out of your control."

As he pulled open the door to the office, the twinge of pain in his back reminded him just how fast circumstances could change. "Believe me, I know I'm not the one in control."

Chloe stepped through the double doors that Jake opened. The room, which looked small from the outside, opened before them. Rows and rows of chairs stretched out before her, but what she noticed was the windows. They were huge, from floor to ceiling, and the view was the magnificent Gulf of Mexico. The ocean churned outside, deep emerald-green framed by crystal-blue sky and dazzling white sand. It was stunning.

She turned to Jake. "How do people pay attention to you when you speak?"

He smiled. "Sometimes they don't, but that's okay. We're here to introduce people to their Creator. What better way than that?"

"The view is breathtaking."

"So many people have expectations of what church should be. I have one simple desire. For our church to be a place where people meet God. That's it. One expectation. That one expectation is met in a bunch of different ways—hospitality, service ministries, small groups—but it all boils down to that one thing."

"And you? What do they get from you?"

His lips twisted into a wry smile. "That's a tougher one. But the same, hopefully. I'm a real person, just like you and everybody else who walks through these doors. I just happen to have my name on the office door."

She looked back at the auditorium. The depth of the room didn't seem to overpower her, maybe because of the warm wood tones, maybe because of the man standing beside her making her feel welcome. It was an interesting thing, to be in such a large room and yet feel at home. "You know I need to ask you a few more questions."

"Okay." The tone of his voice cooled, ice compared to what it had been seconds ago when he'd been talking about his church, his congregation. A reminder that she wasn't one of them, but he faced her, his arms open, his face unguarded.

What kind of man was he? He had big problems. *Huge.* But despite all of that, he had a peace about him that was hard to define. He was hard to peg, and that made her want to dig.

"You want to talk here?"

He shrugged. "Here is fine, or the back entrance to my office is just through those doors."

"All right, let's go somewhere a little more private."

"That doesn't sound good." He gave her a tight smile.

"I want to know more about the days before Julie Mansford's murder. Was there someone new in her life? Any strange phone calls, any friends reappear from the past?"

He held the door to his office open for her to walk through. "I've thought about those things so many times. I've gone over and over it in my mind. You have to remember that I was off my feet for months after the fire. I had nothing to do but replay those last few weeks."

She sat in one of the chairs opposite his desk. "Nothing?"

"Nothing of consequence. I mean, you know, there was the new bag boy at the grocery store, but he moved here with his family—they joined the church not too long after I became the pastor here."

Jake rounded his desk, dropped into his office chair.

Chloe laughed as she noticed the tin on his desk. "Cookies for breakfast, Jake?"

He groaned. "I mentioned in a sermon once that I liked chocolate chip–walnut cookies the best when I was a kid and now I get a tin of them every other day or so. Sometimes more than one and I don't even know who brings them."

Amused, Chloe asked, "How long ago exactly did you mention this cookie fetish?"

"At least four or five months."

When she chuckled, he said, "I'm glad you think it's funny. I've probably gained ten pounds." He reached for a cookie.

She grabbed his hand.

"What?"

Her heartbeat picked up speed as she realized what he'd said. "You said those didn't have a note? You don't know who they're from?"

"I don't know exactly, but it doesn't matter. I know that the tin of cookies is from someone who heard that sermon. It's kind of become the joke around the church, at least among the men."

Her heart beat double-time. "Jake, it does matter. You can't trust anyone—not now."

"Not even you?"

Chloe stared into his eyes for a long minute. She'd like to give him hope that it wasn't someone he knew who was doing this to him, but the odds were good that the perpetrator had crossed his path sometime—somewhere. "Of course you can't. Everyone has an agenda, Jake. Do you know mine?"

Chloe could feel his eyes on her as she slammed out of the room. She crossed the hall to the conference room and found a zippered plastic bag in the tiny kitchenette. When she reentered Jake's office, she found him at the computer with his back turned to the door.

"The questions will have to wait. I need to get these

to the crime lab, Jake. With any luck, they're just eggs, butter, flour and sugar, with a little chocolate thrown in there to make them taste good. But if they're not, this may be the first good clue we've had."

He turned back to face her, his eyes anguished. "I offered Gabe one of those cookies. His wife is expecting a baby in a few months. Am I putting all my friends at risk?"

Chloe tucked the bags under her arm. "I don't think so, Jake, but I don't know. Just…be careful."

He gave a short, quick nod and turned back to the computer.

"Make sure the door is locked when I leave." She hesitated at the door.

Another brief nod was all she got.

The reality of the situation would be setting in if it hadn't already. He was the common factor in two murders and everyone was at risk.

Six hours later, Jake shoved away from his desk. His thoughts, usually coming together on Saturday afternoon, just wouldn't gel. He picked up his coffee mug out of habit, but all that was left was the mud in the bottom. Still, he kept it in his hand as he walked to the window, where he could see the remnants of the sunset, vibrant pink and orange, fading to purple now.

He needed to get home. His sermon wasn't ready but personal experience told him that no matter how much he agonized, he wouldn't put it together tonight. Shadows were deepening in the trees at the edge of the parking lot, making him wonder who might be hiding there. Immediately, he put the cup back on the desk, dismissing the thought along with it. All the talk with Chloe had him on edge.

He wanted to feel safe here, should feel safe here. It was a church. But if he was being systematically stalked and people he cared about were being killed, chances were he was being watched. Someone actually could be watching him right now from the trees.

No longer hesitating, he strode toward the door and reached for the panel that controlled the church's electric system. The lights were on a timer, but he didn't wait for them. He flipped all the switches, flooding the quickly dimming parking lot. Fingers of light stretched into the woods, but he saw nothing. No dark-hooded figure lurked at the edge of the trees with a butcher knife, waiting for him to exit the building.

Feeling ridiculous now, he gathered his sermon notes on the desk and stuffed them into his briefcase. He could try to work more at home. Thinking about Chloe's admonition, he reset the alarm to the church office before he locked the door behind him. Because whether or not someone waited in the woods, there was a killer out there targeting people he cared about, and that person wouldn't hesitate to kill again.

As he reached for the handle to the outside door, he saw the overheads had been left on in a room at the end of the hall. The children's wing hadn't been used today—they could've been left on days ago. He walked down the dark corridor before reaching around the door frame, flipping the switch, plunging the hall into blackness. As he turned back toward his office, Jake resisted the urge to look behind him.

Okay, Lord, I've got the heebie-jeebies, as my mom used to say. I need a reality check.

The sound of banging, slamming, palms slapping on glass startled his pulse into triple-time. He whipped around but saw nothing—no one—at the double doors at the end of the hall.

His heart still galloping in his chest, he started for the door closest to the parking lot. It was probably just teenagers looking for a basketball, or something equally as innocent. He'd let himself get talked into being paranoid. He passed the place where another hall joined this one in a T shape. The banging started again. Like someone locked out of the building and desperately wanting in.

You can't trust anyone. Those had been her last words. Chloe would murder him herself if he let someone in while he was alone here, but he couldn't operate out of fear. It wasn't his way—it never had been. And he wouldn't live his life that way now.

He strode forward to the door to the parking lot and pushed through it, locking it behind him. *Come and get me,* he thought. *Take me.*

If someone wanted him that badly, he could go ahead and kill Jake and be done with torturing his friends. Killing his friends. He wasn't afraid.

He walked slowly toward his red SUV.

"Pastor?"

Jake turned around.

A young woman, maybe nineteen, walked hesitantly toward him. As she got closer, he saw that a baby, around two years old, trailed behind.

"Are you the pastor here?"

"Yes, I'm Jake." He drew a deep breath. "What can I do for you?"

She pulled the tiny kid forward and picked him up. "I'm Anna Prentiss. This little guy is Mason. He's two. He got a little carried away knocking on the door. I'm afraid you might have sticky fingerprints on your glass." Long blond bangs hid her eyes as she ducked her head.

"That's okay. We like kids around here. Can I help you with something, Anna?"

She ducked her head even farther and when she spoke, he could barely hear her. "My boyfriend wanted me to move here. He took off and…I don't have any money to feed Mason." She looked up, eyes brimming. "I don't need anything, I swear. It's just him. If you have a few dollars to spare so I can get him something to eat…"

He pulled his phone out of his pocket and she clutched the little boy tighter, digging a ragged tissue out of her pocket to wipe his runny nose.

"My boyfriend promised he'd found me a job, but I think he was lying."

Jake dialed a number he knew by heart and when Gabe's wife, Sailor, answered, he smiled and put it on speakerphone so Anna could hear. "Hey, Sailor. It's Jake. I'm wondering if you have any of those famous ham sandwiches left in your case. And maybe a fruit cup or two?"

When Sailor laughed and asked if he was hungry, he looked at the young woman and winked. "No, but I've got a lady here with me who happens to be."

When Anna started to protest, Jake held up his hand. "And she's got a cute fella with her who I bet would love some of that warm vanilla milk you make special for little kids."

"Send her over, Jake. I'll get her fixed up. And I don't know if she would mind, but I've got a bunch of day-old scones that I would love for someone to take off my hands. I really hate to throw food away."

When Jake looked back into Anna's face, her eyes were closed and tears were leaking out.

"I think that would be great, Sailor. Thanks."

He hung up the phone. "My friend owns the coffee shop down the street. She was on her own once herself, so don't think you're inconveniencing her. She'll love having you."

Anna pulled the baby in close to her hip. "I don't know how I can repay you."

"If you're looking for work, stop by on Monday. We're always in the market for help in the nursery and from what I can tell, you can handle kids."

Tears spilled out again. "Thank you."

"No thanks necessary. Everybody has tough times. I'm glad we can help." Jake pointed out the coffee shop and watched as she buckled the baby into an old junker of a car.

His phone rang. "Jake Rollins."

"Jake, Chloe Davis. We've got the preliminary report

on those cookies. We haven't had enough time to isolate what was in them, but there was definitely something in there besides the usual ingredients. It's a good thing you didn't eat any."

Just like that, the dread, pain and guilt—yeah, mostly guilt—came roaring back.

"Jake."

"I'm here." He lifted a hand to wave at a brave young woman struggling to survive in a tough world. The old car backfired as she pulled out of the parking lot.

"What was that? Jake! Where are you?"

"I'm still at the church but I'm on my way home."

"Maybe you should stay there and let someone escort you home."

"I'll be seeing my own self home, but thank you for offering, Special Agent Davis. See you at church tomorrow." He hung up the phone. A twinge of guilt slapped on top of the pile he was already carrying around, but he tamped it down. Chloe was a big girl.

There was only so much a person could handle in a day. Jake had reached his limit.

THREE

The church parking area had one space left between an SUV and a minivan in the farthest reaches of the lot. Both were parked as close to the white lines as possible, but Chloe squeezed her Honda into the tiny spot. The last time she'd been to church she'd been eleven and living with her aunt Charlotte and uncle Joe. She loved living there. Charlotte was young and worked at the bank and wore pretty clothes and always smelled sweet. A little like the few memories Chloe had of her own mother.

Chloe smoothed her suit jacket down as inexplicable butterflies jammed their way into her tummy. The sermon that day had been about reaching out to those less fortunate. Chloe had gone home thinking about sharing her dessert with that little girl at school who never had any.

That afternoon, she was sitting on the floor while Aunt Charlotte French-braided her hair. Charlotte told her that she was expecting a baby of her own and that there wouldn't be room for Chloe anymore.

It was the one and only time Chloe had begged to

stay, begged for someone to keep her. She'd jumped to her feet, her braids unraveling everywhere, promising to babysit, to do midnight feedings and change diapers. And when Aunt Charlotte had run crying to the bedroom, Uncle Joe had told her to pack her things and taken her to a group home to live.

That was when she learned that it didn't matter what you did, people took care of themselves first. They might say they loved you, but really…it all came down to them.

As an adult, she could see that her relatives had tried, that maybe they'd done the best they could. She would've done things differently. She climbed the stairs and opened the double doors. The service had already started, but she wanted to observe anyway, to watch from the back and see if anyone stood out, maybe watching too intently, or just didn't fit in with the rest of the crowd.

Even stepping into the room felt like she was trespassing. She didn't belong here. To her surprise, though, the large room didn't feel like the churches she'd visited in the past. A band filled the stage up front by those huge windows she'd seen yesterday and though they played a hymn she thought she recognized, it was different to hear it coming from a rock-and-roll band in jeans and black T-shirts.

Warmly lit hospitality tables at each side of the room overflowed with doughnuts, coffee and juice, making the auditorium feel friendly. Probably by design, like the huge windows, and the worn, rugged wooden cross against the wall at the front of the room.

"Can I help you find a place to sit?" asked a man who towered over her, but the lines in his face slid easily into a smile, making her want to return it.

"No, thanks. I'd really like to stand."

"You're welcome to. Let me know if I can help you with anything." The burly man eased back into the corner, which must be his post.

As Jake took the floor, the band slowly quieted and left the stage. He pulled a stool to the front edge, but had nothing else except his Bible in his hand. When he started speaking, every eye in the place was drawn to him. He spoke simply, but with so much heart that she believed he meant what he said.

He owned the stage, moving across it with a self-assurance that astounded her. She realized she'd been thinking of him as some kind of wounded warrior who turned to this job as an afterthought, but here he was, preaching before a packed house. He was relaxed and easy, confident in a way that had nothing to do with looks and everything to do with ability. As strange as it seemed to Chloe, who had little use for such things, she had little doubt that a higher power was involved here, that God had His hand on this man in this place.

Jake made his point about forgiveness and looked to the back of the auditorium, seeming to look directly into her eyes, even though she knew he probably couldn't see her. It was as if he knew what she was feeling.

Chloe swallowed hard, her bones suddenly seeming too large for her skin. Getting a handle on that man was about as hard as laying hands on a wet cat. She could size a criminal up in two seconds flat, but Jake Rollins defied profiling. She slipped into the lobby and out the double doors to the sidewalk, dragging fresh air into her lungs.

A smartly dressed woman with a short, smooth swing of dark hair carried an armload of manila envelopes up the steps toward the auditorium.

Breathe and focus. She wasn't really here for church, after all. She was here to investigate a murder. "Hi—do you work here?"

The young woman took a pencil out of her mouth, revealing a row of straight white teeth that flashed as she curved her lips into a smile. "I do. Are you lost?"

"No. Actually, I was hoping to ask you a few questions about your boss."

The woman's face shuttered. "I'm sorry. I love working here—and you won't catch me saying anything bad about Pastor Jake or anybody else on staff here."

"I didn't expect you to." Chloe reached into her pocket and flipped open her ID. "I'm Special Agent Davis. I'm helping the local police in an investigation."

Her eyes widened. "I'm Susan Paulson, Pastor Jake's assistant. And I'd shake your hand, but I'm afraid this mountain of attendance files is rather shaky. What's this about?"

"Could you tell me anything that you can remember about Jake Rollins before his fiancée died?"

Jake's assistant tugged her lip between her teeth. "I didn't really know him then. I'd seen him around town and he went to church here, but of course he didn't work here before he was injured."

"Right. Did you know his fiancée?"

Susan shifted the files in her arms. "Yes, but we were all really young. Just getting started, you know? I think she'd just graduated from college and had a job as a teacher. I was working as a secretary at one of the offices in town then."

"Can you think of anything that Julie and Sharon Hardin had in common?"

"Other than being totally gone on Pastor Jake?" The secretary bobbled the files and then recovered. "I shouldn't have said that."

"Jake—Pastor Rollins—said that they were just friends."

"Oh, they were. But that didn't stop Sharon Hardin from telling everyone in town that she was hoping for a June wedding."

"What about you? Have you ever been out with him, or taken a look at him with more than a job in mind?" Chloe had to ask. This woman was probably the one that Jake was the closest to in Sea Breeze, definitely the one he relied on the most.

Susan Paulson flashed what had to be a two-carat diamond engagement ring on the fourth finger of her left hand. "I'm seeing someone. It's strictly platonic between me and Pastor Jake. Like I said, I love working here. A failed relationship between the pastor and his assistant wouldn't exactly make for healthy staff meetings. Anything else?"

With a sinking feeling in her stomach, Chloe thanked Jake's assistant. She had to talk to Jake about

Sharon Hardin. Given this information, the victims had more in common than anyone had known, which meant that the killer was paying closer attention than anyone had suspected.

When Jake walked out the back door by the parking lot, sliding his sunglasses on against the overbright Florida sun, he found Chloe Davis sitting on the bumper of his 4Runner, her face all mashed up into a serious expression. His every muscle screamed for the recliner in his very own living room. Preaching—standing on his feet—for three to four hours in a row was a strain on his already twisted back. But he dredged up a smile anyway, even if just to annoy her. "So, Special Agent Davis, what did you think of our little church?"

"It's not little. And why didn't you tell me the truth about you and Sharon Hardin?"

What small bit of good humor he'd managed vanished like a whiff of smoke. "I did tell you the truth. There was nothing between us." He shoved the words out between clenched teeth and dug his keys out of the pocket of his khakis. "Now if you don't mind, I'm ready to go home."

She pushed off the bumper of his truck and put her hand on the door, effectively blocking his exit. "I do mind. You really can't leave things out or mislead me. It's important, Jake."

"Why is it important to take what little dignity the woman had left away from her? Did you really need to know that she had a crush on me?" He tossed his preaching books onto the passenger seat.

"Yes. Because I'm tracking the victims. *Any* similarities, anything at all makes a difference. It doesn't matter what it *was*. What matters is what our unknown subject *thought* it was. If the unsub overheard Sharon Hardin telling someone she was picking out flowers for a June wedding, guess what he thinks? She's important to you. A target he can take out that will hurt you. Maybe the first in a long time. Maybe since Julie?"

He slumped against the car door, the warmth seeping through his jacket to his skin. "Oh, man. I didn't even consider that."

"You shouldn't have to. But you should tell me everything so I can consider it." She turned to walk away, pulling the strap of her bag up over her shoulder.

"She wasn't really in love with me."

Chloe stopped. Jake didn't know why he wanted her to know this, but it was important that she did.

"Why do you say that?" Chloe's dark brown eyes, so perceptive and so sharp, zeroed in on his.

"It was the idea of me. People see me up on that stage and they think that because I share parts of who I am that it's all that I am. They forget that there's a real flesh-and-blood man that makes up the pastor. And that the man makes mistakes just like they do."

He walked a few steps away and then turned back to her. "Sharon wanted a man who would love and respect her, who wouldn't cheat on her like her ex-husband did. She saw the *kind* of man she wanted to marry in me…not *the* man she wanted to marry." He stabbed his fingers through his hair, making it stand on end. "I'm not making any sense. Sorry. I'm tired."

Chloe reached a hand out to still his restless ones. "No, you're making perfect sense. In fact, you're very perceptive. Now go home. We'll talk later."

"Good idea. I'm brain-dead." He reached for the door handle again, but turned back to her, unable to resist. "Chloe, why did you leave the service in the middle?"

It was the deer-in-the-headlights look she quickly hid that almost had him laughing before he realized that she wasn't anywhere close to finding the question funny. "Hey, I was just messing with you. It's not a big deal."

Her voice was soft but steely. "Don't think that because we're spending time together that you're getting to know me. My faith, or lack thereof, is not any of your business."

"O-kay." He let the word drag out, trying to give her a chance to change her mind. There were obviously some deep-rooted feelings she had that she could use a chance to talk about.

When she didn't, he pulled the door open. "Just think on this, Chloe. We may not be friends, but I've got something you may not think you need, but you want just the same. You think it through and see if that isn't the truth. And when you're ready, you come and see me. We'll talk. Because I may not know a lot, but I know that a gun and badge isn't all there is to life."

He slammed the door and started the engine. Nobody knew better than he did that the job wasn't all there was to life, but most of the time he had a more gracious way of saying it. He peeled out of the parking lot, praying like crazy that, being tired and impatient, he hadn't just messed up and driven Chloe away for good.

Chloe squeezed the steering wheel between her clenched fists. The view out the window should be calming. The sun dipping into the Gulf of Mexico was beautiful. But all she could think of was how she had been rude to Jake earlier, after church—and worse, acted unprofessionally with a witness.

That's what she needed to remember. He was a witness. Nothing more. Even if he did look really good right now sitting on his front steps in a faded SBFD T-shirt, playing that guitar. For sure, the view of the ocean had nothing on him.

She pulled into his driveway. He glanced up, but didn't take his fingers off the frets, just kept up the easy strumming.

When she walked over to him, he didn't say anything. She sat on the step beside him and waited for him to finish the song. The chords he played were uncomplicated and melodic, melding seamlessly with the shushing of the waves across the street. Little by little she felt her muscles unwind from the coil they'd been in all day as she'd worked through the case files, reviewing each and every piece of evidence, looking for any link, any clue. When he started to sing, she closed her eyes and let her head fall back against the wooden post of the porch rail.

He sang a simple worship song, but the words came

from his heart. She knew he believed them in the very core of his being. And that's what made him so attractive. It wasn't the guitar or the broad shoulders under the SBFD shirt, though those were fine…it was *who* he was.

As he played the last chord, he laughed. "Not much of a big finish. My first guitar teacher used to tell me, 'Son, it doesn't matter what you do during the song, if you give them a big finish, that's what your audience will remember.'"

Chloe shoved her hands deeper into the pockets of her jacket, the breeze off the ocean bringing a chill as the sun dipped below the horizon. "Does that work for sermons, too?"

He looked surprised for a minute, then chuckled. "Yeah, I'm pretty sure it does. I hadn't thought about it, but I always try to finish with the most memorable point. So there you go…" He began to strum the guitar again.

"There you go." Wishing she could sit on this front porch forever wasn't getting her any closer to accomplishing what she'd come for. She cleared her throat. "Jake, I was short with you earlier today. It was out of line and I'm sorry."

He missed the chord as his eyes searched for hers. Glancing down at the strings, he picked up the strumming pattern again. "You don't have to apologize. I was tired and wasn't real careful with my words today, either."

"I wanted to explain."

He covered her hand with his, the pick still between his forefinger and thumb. "You're not obliged to explain to me, but if you want to, I want to listen."

"I bounced around a bunch as a kid. A few of the families I lived with tried to take me to church, but it never stuck. It's not that I don't believe in God…"

"You just don't really believe church is the place to find Him."

Shock slammed through her. "How did you know that?"

His brilliant blue eyes were kind. "You're not the first person to feel that way. Let me guess…people thought you should act better, or dress more nicely if you were going to be in church?"

Her eyes stung.

"Let me just give you something to think about, okay?"

If she didn't know better, she would say that he was the behavior specialist. And she wasn't really sure she wanted to hear what he had to say. "Uh, sure?"

"I don't think church is only for perfect, happy people, though if you know any, I'd be glad to recruit them. If you read much of the Bible, you'll see that God's favorite people to use were the least likely. Lepers and tax collectors. I mean, *seriously,* a carpenter and a teenager?"

She sighed, a little exasperated. "Jake."

"Don't say anything. Just think about it."

A siren started up a few blocks away. Jake picked up the guitar and headed into the house.

She followed behind him. "Jake, what's up?"

"Sounds like the fire department. I need to get my cell phone." As he spoke, his phone started ringing. Behind him on the counter, his landline rang, too.

At her hip, Chloe's cell phone buzzed. With foreboding, she silenced it as Jake slammed the phone down and grabbed his keys. "What's wrong? What is it?"

He ran for the door, worry etched on his face. "It was my captain. They've called out all units. Someone set the church on fire."

FOUR

Jake skidded around the corner toward the church. Police had cordoned off the parking lot, but one of the young officers quickly rolled back the yellow tape so he could enter. A crowd had gathered outside the barrier.

Chloe sat silently in the passenger seat beside him. Probably scared for her life the way he'd been driving. He shoved the gearshift into Park and opened the door. "I don't know how long I'll be."

"Go. I'll be fine. I've got some work to do here." She pulled a digital camera out of her bag.

He started to get out of the car, but looked back. "Chloe, be careful."

He couldn't tell what she was thinking. Her eyes were shadowed in the darkness, the flashing red lights giving everything a weird, familiar glow.

She nodded. "I will, I promise. Now go."

Three fire trucks had pulled up in front of the church and two more were around the side of the building. Hoses in seemingly random patterns crisscrossed the ground and firefighters worked the fire in a well-choreographed dance. The parking lot lights were out, but someone on the crew would have turned off the electricity at the main circuit board, trying to avoid secondary fires.

He shoved his way through the crowd of cops and paramedics to find the captain. Emergency lights switched on, but the smoke still made it hard to see. Jake's eyes burned with tears as he pushed toward the building that housed his office.

Matt Clark grabbed his arm, pulling him away from the church. "Hey, bro. It's not as bad as it looks."

"It looks bad, Matt."

Matt shrugged a shoulder across his cheek and only succeeded in swiping more soot across the surface. "It's mostly smoke. The fire had multiple points of origin, but no accelerant. I think they must have been set off electronically."

Jake closed his eyes, his shoulders sagging. "The church is okay?"

Matt hesitated. "It will be."

"Where did the fires start?"

"There was one in each wing. One in the worship center under the stage. Small explosives, probably. We won't have more information until we sift through all the evidence. And that's going to have to wait until tomorrow."

"Thanks, Matt." He glanced behind him at the multiplying crowd. "I need to get back there and let people know that the church building will be okay."

Jake silently breathed a prayer of thanks. He knew how lucky they were. Structure fires, especially as large as this one, with multiple points of access and origin, were notoriously difficult to fight. And with no one inside, if the building had been too far gone, it wouldn't be worth risking the lives of the firefighters. Their efforts would have been focused on controlling the blaze to keep it from spreading to other places—nearby houses and businesses along the boardwalk.

For what seemed like hours, he moved from person to person, reassuring each one that while there was damage, it could be repaired. His throat ached from the smoke and talking. It was like his worst night on the job as fire chaplain, but times one hundred, because so many cared what happened to the church. For all these people, it became a home, maybe the only real place many felt welcomed and loved. And because he understood it, he needed to reach out to them.

Icy-cold water slid down his arm. When he turned, Chloe held out a dripping Diet Coke. "Thought you could use this."

"You have no idea." He cracked it open and nearly groaned in relief as the frosty liquid eased the dryness in his throat.

"Are you about finished here?"

He looked around. The crowd, mostly church members, had dwindled as word got out that the church would survive and everything would be fine. "I guess I can slip away and run you back to your car. I'm sorry that you've had to stay here all night."

"That's not why I was asking." She held out her camera. "I took a lot of pictures tonight, at least a couple hundred. Can you help me find somewhere to print them?"

"Am I missing something? Why do you need pictures of the church from tonight?"

"I took pictures of the people. If you'll look at them and identify the ones you know, while you do that, I can study the body language and facial expressions, looking for something that doesn't fit. I don't think the arsonist would be able to hide his expression, especially if he didn't think anyone was watching."

"I think there's an all-night copy place in town. They probably have a computer and printer setup we can use."

Chloe turned and walked toward the car, her red hair swinging behind her with every step. He watched her walk away, excitement over the possibility of a lead overwhelmed by bone-deep weariness, and a new thought that had him frozen in place.

Near his car, she turned back. "You coming?"

He'd known almost every person in the crowd tonight. They were people who'd been in his Bible studies and listened to his sermons. Church members, coworkers and neighbors. What if, by identifying a possible arsonist, he was pointing a finger at a friend?

Her eyes closed, Chloe rolled her shoulders, trying to maneuver the kinks out of her back and neck. She and Jake had been at this for hours, first in the car outside the copy shop and now at Sip This. They'd been waiting outside when Sailor got there to bake, and, taking pity on them, she'd given them a table, even though she hadn't been open yet.

Jake had studied each photo, identifying the faces in the

hundreds of shots she'd taken at the crime scene tonight. And there was little doubt that it was a crime scene.

CSI Maria Fuentes and her team would be there at daylight combing through the evidence, but no one believed that the fire at the church had been started by natural causes. Four points of origin in four different wings of the building—it wasn't accidental.

At the smell of wonderful, fresh-ground, liquid caffeine, she snapped her eyes open. Gabe Sloan stood just out of arm's reach with two mugs of coffee. "I've been up all night and I carry a gun, Gabe. Are you really sure you want to hold the coffee hostage?"

He laughed and handed her a cup. "You're quite a negotiator."

"It worked, didn't it?" She pulled the mug close, cupping the warm ceramic in her hands.

Jake snagged the other one from Gabe and took a big swallow. "You're a lifesaver, Sloan."

"Thank Sailor. She's baking scones, too. If you're nice, you can have one."

Jake cocked an eyebrow at Chloe. "I think between the two of us, we could take him out."

"You know it." She grinned. "We just have one more set of pictures to go through."

She flipped open the manila folder.

Jake pushed back from the table, slapping a hand flat over the photos. "No. There's no way any of those guys had anything to do with this. They wouldn't do that, not to the church and not to me. Chloe, they come to church on Sunday morning, bringing the rig and everything."

Chloe tugged the hair band out of her hair with an impatient twist. "Jake, statistically speaking, it's not that unlikely that it would be a firefighter, especially since the building was unoccupied at the time the fire started…and with what's been going on lately, I don't think we can rule anyone out. Let's make sure this fire is related to the others."

She looked to Gabe for help. He shrugged and turned toward the kitchen, obviously wanting to stay away from this discussion.

Jake leaned over the table, his shoulders tense. "It's not one of my crew."

"Probably not, but will you at least look at the pictures?" Chloe glanced around. Customers had started to trickle in and she didn't want their conversation overheard. Maybe it was time to call it a night and give Jake a rest.

Gabe slid a plate of still-steaming scones onto the table and said, "After breakfast—it's been a long night, Jake. Look at the pictures after you eat."

"Fine. Chloe?" Traces of bluish-gray circles underlined his vivid blue eyes.

She stared into them. He was exhausted and needed a break. She could give him that much. "Fine."

Chloe stifled the irrational urge to shove a whole scone in her mouth and call it done. She broke off a small piece of the warm bread and popped it in her mouth. "Oh, wow."

Gabe grinned. "Yeah, that's what I said the first time I had one of Sailor's pastries. And then I decided to marry her." He walked back toward the kitchen. "Play nice now, children."

Jake ate silently for a moment before saying, "Tell me more about this body language thing. How does it work?"

She thought for a second, then pointed at a couple sitting at a table across the room. "See those two? The ones wearing the SBFD shirts? Do you know them?"

He nodded. "Matt Clark and Lara Hughes."

"It's not a stretch to assume they work together, right?"

He tilted his head, acknowledging her statement.

"But there's more to that relationship than just working together."

Jake started to interrupt, but she held up her hand. "Give me a second. See how he's leaning in to her? He wants her to see him. She's looking away slightly. He even has his hands on the table, but hers are in her lap and she has the coffee cup between them, shielding her midsection. She doesn't want him to see *her.*"

Jake narrowed his eyes, considering. "That just means they're having an intense conversation, not necessarily that they have feelings for each other."

"Yeah, but see how he's rolling that cup back and forth in his hands? He's a little nervous, but he's doing something tactile with his hands. He's thinking about her." She shrugged. "I've had pretty consistent results using body language as criteria."

As they watched, Matt Clark drilled his fingers into his hair and Lara Hughes shoved away from the table, stalking to the coffeepot with her mug.

Chloe looked at Jake.

A reluctant grin pulled at his lips. "Maybe you're right."

The trickle of customers that had been in and out since the early-morning hours had suddenly turned into a rush. The line snaked through the tables. Even though they were in the corner, curious eyes scanned the stack of file folders. Chloe picked them up and stuffed them into her messenger bag. "So, you want to get out of here?"

"I could use some fresh air."

No less than twelve people stopped Jake to talk on the way out the door. Finally on the front steps, Chloe breathed a sigh of relief. "Is it always like that for you?"

"Like what?"

"Everybody wants to talk to you." She barely repressed a shudder. Give her the anonymity of the city any day.

Jake looked genuinely surprised. "Yeah, I guess. If I don't know people from church, then I know them from a civic committee or from being the fire chaplain."

He took her elbow, leading her toward the boardwalk. She slung her bag over her shoulder, following him down the long wooden walkway toward the sand. "Doesn't it get exhausting?"

"Maybe, sometimes. But I'm used to it, and I like knowing what's going on in people's lives."

She stopped, looked at him. "You date any of them?"

"What does that have to do with anything?" He tugged her with him to keep walking.

"At least three of those women were trying to get you to ask them out." She wasn't jealous, just a little miffed and definitely curious.

Now he froze, his mouth gaping. "You're crazy."

"I was right about your firefighter friends. Matt and Lara?" She didn't stop with him, just turned to walk backward.

"Being right once doesn't mean you're right about this."

"Okay." She put her hands up. "Backing off."

He rolled his eyes up like maybe he was praying for patience as he started walking toward her. "Are you asking me a serious question or are you just trying to embarrass me?"

"Serious." But she tucked away the fact that he was embarrassed by the attention.

Jake was silent for a few steps as he caught up with her on the rough boardwalk. "It's crazy the way the older women try to play matchmaker. But there have only been a couple of girls I was even remotely interested in. Sailor's the only one I asked out. After a couple of dates, we decided we were just friends, and—"

He came to a hard stop, spinning around to face the ocean, placing his hands flat on the railing of the boardwalk. "I can't believe I've been so stupid."

She put her hand on his arm. "Jake, what is it?"

"You were there." He turned his head toward her, his blue eyes burning with intensity as he searched hers.

"When?"

"Her house caught on fire. Remember? She wasn't there, but you were almost trapped in the blaze. We all assumed that Sailor's house was torched because of the case she was involved in, but it was never proved. And now…"

"Now we need access to those files." Chloe pulled her phone out, pressing the numbers for Gabe Sloan. Because if there was one related fire, chances were good there were more.

In the fire department's central office, Jake rubbed his eyes. Too much smoke, too little sleep. He tossed another file on the pile of unexplained cases. Four new fires, each with similarities to the fire in the church and the one at Sailor's house. None with the organization of the crimes that killed Julie and Sharon Hardin.

But his captain was right. With every fire they fought, the probability increased that someone on his crew would get hurt. Too many call-outs and too little time to recover created a dangerous situation for the fire department.

Maria Fuentes pulled a hair band off her wrist and secured her springy brown curls into a loose ponytail on top of her head. "This just doesn't make sense. We've got the fire that kills Julie, then the fire at Sailor's house, which I guess could have been meant to kill her. But there was no evidence that those two were started by the same person…unless you add the arson at the church, and that opens a whole new can of *clostridium botulinum*."

Gabe Sloan tossed another file onto the pile and smirked at Maria. "He kills once, then doesn't, then kills again in the Sharon Hardin case? Could a killer that organized be that erratic?"

Chloe had been awake as long as Jake had, but she still managed to look fresh, even though she'd shed her suit coat hours ago to reveal a white tank top. "Most killers have a pattern, but unless the pattern is random just to throw us off…"

"There is no pattern. Maybe his goal is making me confused, and if so, it's working." Jake slid another file over to Maria.

"Thanks bunches, Friar Tuck, because I really need more evidence to sift through."

"No problem. I'm happy to help." Jake grinned at Maria.

The feisty CSI made a face back at him, another reason he admired her. She didn't treat him like he was any different from any other person. Some people clammed up when they found out he was a pastor. Others never got beyond basic civility, fearing, he guessed, that if their pastor knew they were real people with real problems he might not let them back into church. If they only knew.

Maria stood, straightened the kinks out of her back and reached for the stack of files. "I'm going to start pulling the evidence logs on these. If you come across any more, fax them over to me."

"Will do. Thanks, Maria." As the door closed behind Maria, Chloe dropped into a chair. "I don't like this. Without a clear pattern, it's really difficult to come up with a profile."

Gabe stood and moved toward the door. "It seems like we're not getting anywhere, but we're further than we were yesterday. Don't give up. I've got to get back to the station."

Jake's phone beeped. He scrolled through the screens

to a new text message from his assistant. "I've got to go to the hospital. One of our members had a heart attack this morning. Can I drop you off somewhere?"

Chloe looked longingly at the door, but shook her head and pulled another stack of files toward her. "No, I'm going to finish up here. Talk to you later?"

"You bet." He closed the door behind him as he left the office. Leaving Chloe at the fire station was safe. The guys were there 24/7. So why did he feel like he was abandoning her?

Who was he kidding? By her own admission, Chloe Davis was used to working on her own, usually in the middle of the bad guys with no backup. She definitely didn't need him.

"I don't think we need the team. Not yet." Her cell phone glued to her ear, Chloe paced the length of the beach house that she'd rented, thankful at least to be in jeans and barefoot instead of work clothes and heels. "But, sir, I'm going to be here a few more days, at least. Right now we've got a mishmash of possibly connected crimes, two deaths and no real profile of a suspect."

Her boss, distant on a good day, seemed even more disconnected over the cell phone. "You have good instincts, Davis. Who do you think is doing the crimes?"

She hesitated, knowing she could be risking her fledgling career in the behavioral sciences division. "I think our unsub may be a woman."

"Statistically that's unlikely. Arsonists are almost always male."

"Unless revenge is the motive." She took a deep breath. "If you look at the crime-scene photos, the victims' personal items are burned. I think that suggests retribution of some kind."

"Why aren't the bodies burned?" Her boss didn't exactly sound like he was buying into her theory.

"That's more about the killer being proud of the work. She doesn't want her artwork, this tableau she's set, to be destroyed." Chloe forced herself to sit, her gaze landing on her landlord's lime-green beach house two doors down.

"An arsonist who kills is almost always a loner, someone who would stand out in a normal crowd. He was probably abused as a child."

She bounced back to her feet, unable to sit still. "Couldn't that apply to a woman, as well?"

"It could. It just usually doesn't." She could hear his pencil tapping on his desk, a sign of annoyance he usually reserved for the techs.

"What about the pastor?"

She nearly slipped and said, *"Jake?"*

Catching herself, she floundered for a few seconds. "He was cleared in the first crime. He was on duty at the firehouse with his crew when the fire was set and was injured trying to get to his fiancée in time to save her."

"He could be a fit for the new crimes. Maybe that's why the long stretch between kills. He was getting up the nerve, prepping, rehearsing. I read in your report that he has all the case notes from the first case. Former fire-fighter, looking for the adrenaline rush. Statistically it wouldn't be out of the realm of possibility."

"Respectfully, sir, I think you're wrong here." Warm, she pulled her hair off her neck in a makeshift ponytail.

"Chloe, be careful. If you feel that your judgment is getting clouded by personal connections, remember that you have a team now. You don't have to do this on your own anymore. In fact, I really don't recommend it."

If that was a veiled threat, she certainly felt it in the pit of her stomach. "I spent a lot of time undercover, sir. I've never let any personal relationships get in the way of bringing down the target."

He cleared his throat and seemed to hesitate. "You know as well as I do that a person can kill another human being in the most depraved way possible and then go home and hug his kids. It doesn't make sense, but it happens. Don't let this case be the one that ends your career because you were too close to see the truth."

"Yes, sir." Chloe snapped her phone shut and stared at the patio door. Her reflection stared back at her. Her famous instincts were deserting her. What she needed was some good old-fashioned police work. Evidence and facts—those things were familiar, reassuring and incontrovertible. Maybe a nap would help.

Beyond the doors, the Gulf of Mexico shushed against the sand, an endless flow of water against the shore. She'd been on her own for so long, worked alone for so long. Why did that sound suddenly make her feel lonely? Even the brightly painted walls of the beach house failed to cheer her.

Could be this town was finally getting to her—the people here knew each other and really seemed to care about each other. The crowd at the church last night had been a perfect example of that. At least a dozen men had called Jake today while they were going through the files to offer their help when the church was deemed safe for cleanup.

And maybe she'd stayed too long in the undercover world because she had a hard time believing that people were that nice, that they didn't have their own motives for doing good things. Like she'd told Jake, everyone had an agenda.

A knock on the door startled Chloe. She lifted her weapon from the end table where she'd left it in easy reach and strode to the door, taking a quick peek through the window. Jake's truck sat in the driveway.

She put the gun away and opened the door. "How'd you know where to find me?"

He gave her a look. "It's a small town. By breakfast, everybody and their first cousin will know you're renting from our esteemed police lieutenant and his new wife." He held out a white plastic bag. "I brought you a present."

Chloe pulled out a pink T-shirt with a big red cartoon crab on the front. "I Got Crabby at Sea Breeze Beach. Cute."

"Well, I couldn't help but notice that it was particularly appropriate." Jake walked into the great room, but shot her a smile over his shoulder.

"I'm not crabby. I'm tense. Alert. There's a difference." She stalked into the kitchen for the lighter wand and clicked it on, lighting her sugar-cookie-scented candles.

The candles made the impersonal hotel rooms and condos she always seemed to be living in smell like a home.

"Uh-huh." He made himself comfortable on her couch.

"What are you doing?"

He didn't answer her, just popped back to his feet and roamed around the beach house, fingering the small beachy touches that her landlord had placed around. Baskets of shells, three starfish in a line, a bowl of sea glass. "How do you feel about Chinese food?"

She narrowed her eyes. "Chinese food and I are friendly. Was there a point to your visit, Jake?"

He stopped walking, shoved his hands in the pockets of his faded denims and turned the power of those vivid blue eyes on her. "I wanted to see you."

She fought the urge to swallow hard. "About the case?"

"That, and I don't know, Chloe…is it so hard to believe that I might just like you as a person?"

The two of them were so different, but maybe it wasn't a stretch to imagine that he was lonely tonight, too. He'd had a really hard week. She tossed him the phone. "General Tso's chicken."

He grinned. "Coming up."

Maybe her boss was right, because when Jake turned the power of those blue eyes and that dimple on her, she didn't want to believe he could be guilty of anything more than a traffic violation. And keeping her objectivity had sometimes been the only thing that kept her alive.

FIVE

Jake raked beef and broccoli into his mouth as Chloe tossed her chopsticks into the empty carton on the table on the back deck. The woosh of the rolling surf beyond was their only dinner music, save the occasional screech of gulls determined to steal some of his fried wontons.

"I'm so full." Chloe propped one foot on the chair opposite her, pale pink polish on her toenails. Jake stared. He wouldn't have guessed the very capable Chloe to be a pink-polish girl. The thought was intriguing. She had layers that he hadn't discovered yet.

When she sighed, he gestured at the ocean with his chopsticks, a dangling piece of broccoli in danger of hitting the table. He ignored it. "It's good for what ails you. Have you dipped your toes in?"

She blinked. "The water temp's in the fifties."

"Won't kill ya. Come on." He held out a hand.

Though she allowed him to pull her up, he couldn't help but think she could have him on his stomach with his hand pinned behind him in two seconds flat.

For some reason, it made him smile. He flipped his shoes into the sand at the bottom of the stairs. She sent him a hard look and rolled her jeans up.

"Oh, come on. You're the one who's been barefoot all night."

"I've had three-inch heels on all day." She stepped off into the sand. "Ooh."

Now that the sun had dropped, the silky-smooth sand was cold, molding to the contours of his feet. "Feels good, doesn't it?"

Without looking at her, he took her hand and began to walk. The sun, orange-red against the lush purple sky, began to dip into the dark ocean. "So, you were in foster care. Is this something I should know about? Were you some kind of delinquent at the age of seven?"

She snickered. "I would've been a good delinquent."

He didn't mind that she didn't jump straight into the truth. Sometimes it took people a while to open up to him because of the pastor thing. Maybe they thought he'd be sending a scorecard up to the Lord every night or something. Somehow he suspected that wasn't the issue with Chloe. She just didn't open up. Period.

He heard her take a deep breath. "My parents died when I was in kindergarten. I was sent to live with my grandparents first. I was pretty precocious, didn't mind very well. So they sent me to live with my aunt. Between my parents, they had seven brothers and sisters. I lived with all of them."

The words were matter-of-fact, but the pain was still there. He could hear it in her voice. Jake turned her toward him. "Sounds like you were hurting. A little girl looking for what you had lost. I'm sorry."

She swallowed hard, pushed away from him and kept walking, a little faster.

Chloe stooped to the rolling surf to pick up a glass bottle and kicked through the sand to the nearest trash can. Soft, damp air wrapping around him, Jake waited, if not patiently then stubbornly, wanting to know more about her. He wasn't willing for this to be one of those relationships that just skimmed the surface.

Her lip caught in her teeth, she walked back to him, but she didn't pick up his hand. He wasn't offended. They walked a couple of minutes back toward her house, the only sound the soft swish of the ocean against the sand.

"My parents died in a fire."

He stopped, his feet squeaking in the cool damp sand. "How did it happen?"

"I'm really not sure. I tried to get the file once, but it was a long time ago. Before computer files were the norm." Her face held no hint of the little girl she'd been then. "My dad got me out of the house first. He went back for my mom and they didn't make it out."

Other than a tiny catch in her voice, he would never have known that it mattered to her. Because she'd been schooled over and over again that you couldn't depend on people to be there, she'd taught herself not to care. He heard stories of heartbreak every day, but he'd never once wanted to take the people he counseled into his arms and tell them it was all going to be okay, not like he wanted to with Chloe.

"Does it bother you, working fire scenes?"

"No." She stepped away. "I'm cold. I'm going in."
She ran up the stairs.

"I'll be there in a few." He sat on the stairs to watch the
last of the brilliantly colored clouds disappear. Chloe was
pulling away from him. The steps were just a physical way
to mark the space that she'd already shoved between them.

He took a deep breath of the sea-salty air, letting it
fill him, renew him. The ocean, as always, reminded him
of God's power. God's constant presence and His
unending love.

Brushing the sand off his jeans, he stood to follow
Chloe. On the deck, he picked up his chopsticks and her
half-empty box of General Tso's chicken. "So what do
you want to do tonight?"

"I need to work, Jake." She stopped stacking the
empty boxes.

Not just pulling away, putting up a barrier that the
Jaws of Life couldn't slice through. He'd gotten too
close, too fast. At least for Chloe. But he couldn't bring
himself to be sorry that he'd gotten a glimpse into what
made her who she was.

Gathering the last of the boxes, he slid the glass patio
door open with his foot.

She was popping the top on a Diet Coke.

"Preparing for a long night?"

"There's got to be some clue somewhere that I'm not
seeing." Pictures of the crime scenes were spread out on
the table beside her laptop. A magnifying glass lay on
top of them.

He crossed to the kitchen and tossed the boxes in the white plastic can. Tying the bag up, he smiled at her.

She pressed her lips together, obviously fighting a battle whether to talk to him or kick him out. The need for his input about townspeople versus her need to be on her own.

"There are a few people in the photos that I've identified at each crime scene. I want to get your impression of them. Maybe they're just curious onlookers, maybe there's some other motive for being there. It's possible you'd know what that is."

He hoisted the bag. "I'll take a look after I take your trash out."

She wasn't used to being cared for. Why he felt the need to show her what it felt like, he had no idea. It was a recipe for heartbreak for sure, but something about her story, about that little girl lost, got to him. Maybe he identified too much.

The night air, while warm for late January, still carried a chill in the breeze off the Gulf of Mexico. He tossed the bag into the big trash can and stepped back, bumping into someone as he did.

"Oh!" Jerking earbuds out of her ears, the woman, in running clothes and trainers, had a baseball cap pulled low over short, streaky blond hair, but he thought he recognized her from church.

He did know her. Third row, left side. "Elaine?"

"Wha— Oh. *Pastor?*"

"You can call me Jake, Elaine. What are you doing out here?"

"I run the beach road, or sometimes along the bay front in town. It's a much better view than my place." She fiddled with the cord from her iPod, not looking him in the eyes.

"I hear you there." He shoved his hands into his jeans pockets to warm them. "Well, good to see you, Elaine."

"Yeah, you, too, Past—um—Jake." She smiled shyly as she tucked her earbuds back in her ears. "See you around."

He watched her uneven gait settle into a solid run. She looked back once as she reached the next turn, lifting her hand in a small wave before disappearing from sight.

Something nagged at him about her. Maybe it was just that he should have made more of an effort with her. She'd called him when she'd first joined the church. He'd suggested some areas where she might plug into fellowship and given her name to the volunteer coordinator but as far as he knew, she hadn't joined in any activities.

She'd enjoy the church more if she participated, but he couldn't force people into relationships. They had to do that on their own terms, in their own time. Just like he couldn't force one very stubborn woman to open up to him.

Jake started up the stairs to the house, mentally preparing himself for the crime-scene photos. It wasn't easy seeing Sharon Hardin's house and the church. Seeing them in the context of Julie's murder was even harder.

He pushed the door open. "Chloe?"

"Still here." She had her computer on the coffee table

beside the photos, which were divided into four stacks from the four crime scenes they knew they could connect to Jake. His stomach turned. Just the thought of that made him sick. Julie. Sailor. Sharon. His church. What or who would be next?

Could he be putting Chloe in danger just by spending time with her? Why hadn't he thought of that? "I've got to get home."

"What? We haven't even started yet." She looked at him then. "Jake, what is it?"

He reached for his keys on the kitchen counter. "Nothing. I just realized it's better for you if I go."

Her lips lifted, a small smile. "In so many ways, you're right. But I'm a big girl and a trained FBI agent. I can take care of myself. If you think you're putting me at risk by being here, forget it."

Since that was exactly what he had been thinking, he went to the refrigerator and pulled out a Diet Coke, popping the top only to stare at it.

"I'm serious, Jake. Forget it. You're not responsible for my safety. In fact, I'm responsible for yours."

"Okay, I get it. You're a big strong cop, and I'm just along for the ride." He swigged from the can of Coke and wiped his mouth off with the back of his hand.

"Stop being a baby." She waved the photos at him. "Come help."

"Well, when you put it that way…" He rolled his eyes at her as he walked to the couch, settling beside her and tossing fortune cookies onto the coffee table. "Show me what you found."

She scooted closer to him and pulled her computer onto her lap. "I looked through all of these in hard copy and then went to the digitals. It'll be easier for you to see on the screen."

Three squares flashed onto the screen, two men and a woman. Three suspects?

"Do you know these people?"

"That one, the balding guy? He's a lawyer. His name is Fortner. Steve Fortner, I think. I don't know if he always goes to crime scenes, but I'd guess he has a scanner in his car, maybe his office, too."

She pointed to the next one, a woman. "I think I saw her at your church Sunday."

He felt a little sick and put the Diet Coke on the side table. "You did. She sings backup in the band."

"What does she do for work?"

"Bank teller at Opportunity, that bank on the corner as you come into town." He didn't want to help anymore. These people were his friends. Did he really want to know that one of them was a murderer? "I don't know if I can do this."

"I know it's hard. This is your community. But one of these people is targeting you. Very likely someone who lives here and works here. It may not be one of these...but if these people were there, maybe they'll remember something that will help."

He nodded and pointed at the other picture. "I don't know him. Believe it or not, there are some people in town I don't recognize."

"It's pretty weird that he would've been at the scene

after Julie was killed, at Sailor's house, at Sharon Hardin's house and at the church." She scribbled a note on a piece of paper and tucked it into a file folder.

"Seems so." Jake wanted to run, like he'd just seen Elaine doing. Get out on the beach in his tennis shoes and go for miles, escaping from the demons that seemed determined to catch up with him here. Running was another thing the fire had taken away from him. The beam that had fallen on him as he tried to rescue Julie had damaged his spine. No high-impact sports allowed.

So he was no Lance Armstrong, but he'd logged quite a few miles on his bike since he'd recovered enough to ride. He had a feeling he'd be out tomorrow morning— he needed it.

"We'll keep looking. There's one more that I was saving for last. See this one? It's the crowd scene from the church. I didn't see anyone in the group of onlookers here that were at Sharon's house until… See this little scrap of red here?"

Chloe pointed at a tiny triangle on the photo. When he nodded, she clicked a button. "I blew it up and enhanced it with the tools I have. We can do better if I send it to one of the techs at Quantico. But see what I got?"

When he looked closer, a face appeared out of the grainy dots. "That's amazing."

"Do you recognize her?"

"I'm not sure."

Chloe pulled up another photograph. "Here she is again at the Sharon Hardin crime scene. Almost invisible she's so far in the background. But when I blow it up…"

The face clicked into focus, much clearer than the last one because the photos had been taken in the daylight. He recognized the ball cap first and sucked in a breath. "That's Elaine Barbury. I was just talking to her outside."

"What?" Chloe grabbed his sleeve and pulled him closer, the better to get in his face. "Why didn't you say anything?"

"I didn't think about it. Elaine said she was out for a run. People run or walk here all the time, even when they don't live on the beach."

"Or she could've arranged to run into you."

"I guess." He picked up his Diet Coke. "She's not really the homicidal-maniac type."

"And you know the homicidal type so well."

His stomach plummeted. He brushed the condensation off the aluminum can. "Obviously not if someone I know has been targeting me by taking aim at people I care about."

"Jake." When he looked at her, her face had softened and she looked almost like someone who would understand.

He touched a piece of long auburn hair that had fallen out of her ponytail to curl softly at her temple.

She stared into his eyes. The space between them was only a few inches, but it may as well have been a mile. "I'll have these three brought in to interview tomorrow. Hopefully they'll know something that points us in the right direction."

"I'm going to say good-night." With his free hand,

he reached for a fortune cookie and handed it to her. "But I can't leave until you open your cookie."

"Come on, Jake, that's silly." When he refused to get off the couch, she pulled the wrapper off the cookie and cracked it open. "'To achieve a great goal, one must begin with a small achievement.'"

He leaned back against the cushions of the solid-white couch. "Well, I think we've done that tonight. We've got a starting place at least, people to question."

"Open yours."

He cracked the tiny cookie and pulled the slip of paper into his hand, straightening it with his fingers. He glanced at her sideways, wondering, what if? Yeah, he should go for it. He'd always been a little bit of a rebel. Always the one through the door first, always the one to take a chance.

"'Kiss the girl sitting next to you.'" He looked into her deep brown eyes, the color of rich, dark chocolate.

Chloe blinked long and slow, and couldn't quite hide her reaction as her eyes dilated. He let the smile deepen.

Her lips softened, parted. Her eyes closed and for a split second, he imagined she drifted toward him.

She opened her eyes and he faced the FBI stare.

"O-*kay*, kidding. Wow, I wouldn't want to be the guy sitting across the table from you in an interrogation. Mine says, 'The time is right to make new friends.'"

"Give me that." She snatched it out of his hand.

He chuckled. "You can go put that 'crabby' shirt on when I leave."

"You can go soak your head."

"I like you, Davis. I think we *are* going to be friends." He stood and reached for her hand, pulling her to her feet, bringing her within inches of his face. Her scent, like warm vanilla sugar, teased him. She fidgeted. He skimmed his knuckles across her cheek, not even really sure why.

Instead of waiting to see if she'd reach for her service weapon, he reached for the doorknob. As prickly as she could be, he saw a softer side of Chloe Davis—the side that painted her toenails pink and lit candles in houses that didn't belong to her. A side that really needed a trustworthy friend.

Outside, he opened the door to his 4Runner and slid in, realizing as he did so that any relationship between them was impossible. Because no matter what she said about being a trained cop, the more he liked Chloe, the more he placed her in danger.

SIX

Chloe closed the door to the interview room with an audible click. Her third and last interview of the day. The smell of fear and distrust hung in the room, not to mention the stale station house coffee that Gabe kept bringing her.

Elaine Barbury sat across the table from her. "Ms. Barbury, I'm S.S.A. Chloe Davis with the FBI. You already know Detective Gabe Sloan of the SBPD. You're not under suspicion of any crime at this time. We're only here to ask you a few questions. Okay?"

The blond woman's highlight-streaked hair bobbed as she nodded her head, looking back and forth between the two cops. "Do I…need a lawyer?"

Gabe spoke from his position leaning against the institutional gray wall. "All we're looking for is information right now, Elaine. There's nothing to worry about."

"Sure. Okay." She still didn't meet their eyes, instead focusing on twisting and untwisting her fingers on the stainless table.

"What were you doing at the scene the night of the church fire?"

Elaine Barbury's eyes snapped to Chloe's and slid immediately away. "There were a lot of people there that night."

"I know. I've interviewed some of them. Why were *you* there?"

"We were all worried about the church and…" Her voice trailed off.

"And what, Elaine?"

"And Pastor Jake."

She wanted to ask Elaine about her "relationship" with Jake but didn't dare risk her clamming up. Yet. "But what about the other fires?"

This time Elaine kept her eyes on her hands. "What other fires?"

Chloe pulled the photos out and laid them one by one on the table. "Sharon Hardin. Sailor Sloan. Julie Mansford." She pointed to each grainy shot. "There you are at each crime scene trying to fade into the background. But I saw you."

Elaine didn't say anything, her mouth pulled into a frown.

"What were you doing there, Elaine?"

"It's not illegal, is it? To go where there are fires and emergency people? My dad was an EMT."

"So?" She didn't get the reference.

"My mom and I used to go sometimes if there was a call-out. To watch."

Gabe walked to the edge of the table. "Do you like to start fires, Elaine?"

"I don't know why you'd ask me a question like that." Her eyes filled with tears.

Chloe stepped into the conversation. "What about Jake, Elaine? Do you like Jake?"

"Yes…no. I mean, he's my pastor. He's a good man, I think." She blinked hard.

Gabe leaned over the table. His voice was gentle. "Elaine, would you like to have more than a friendly relationship with Jake?"

Her cheeks flushed red and her head dipped even farther toward her hands, her bobbed blond hair sliding forward to cover her face. "I can't answer that."

Chloe closed her file. "I think you just did. Elaine, can you tell me where you were between the hours of five o'clock and eight o'clock, just before the fire started?"

"At my house." She whispered it.

"Can anyone corroborate your story?" Chloe tried to make eye contact, but the shy woman did not lift her eyes from the table.

"My cat." There was an edge to Elaine's laugh. "Are you sure I don't need a lawyer?"

"One more question. Do you believe in revenge?"

Elaine lifted her face to stare at Chloe, her gaze sharpening. "You mean, an eye for an eye, a tooth for a tooth, like that?"

Chloe resisted the frisson of excitement that ran up her spine. "Yeah, like that."

Elaine sat back in her chair; the shy woman who'd barely been able to get words out was gone. "I do. But if you're trying to pin these fires on me as revenge, that's not my style. I like Jake. And believe me, Miss Special Agent—" She made her hands into the shape of a gun. "If I wanted to get even with somebody, he'd never see it coming."

Chloe forced herself to sit still and stay silent, to let the two-faced woman continue, even though her heart raced.

Elaine paused, looked between the two cops. "I think I'll be calling that lawyer now."

"Actually, we're through here." Chloe pushed her chair back from the table as Gabe and Elaine Barbury both snapped their eyes to Chloe. "I'll contact you if I need to ask you any more questions."

Gabe opened the door to the interview room. "Sergeant Sheehan, would you please escort Ms. Barbury down to her car?"

The sergeant opened the door wide to allow Elaine Barbury to precede him down the hall. Closing the door behind them, Gabe turned to Chloe. "She would've told you more if you'd pushed harder."

"Maybe. I don't think she's our girl." She caught Gabe's quick look and chose her words more carefully. "If in fact we're looking for a female, I don't think she fits the profile. Did you see how she changed her behavior when we asked about revenge? This is not a strange notion to her. We need to dig into her background, but watching her eyes and her natural hand gestures, I don't think she was lying when she described how she would do it. I think she was nervous before because she genuinely likes Jake."

"Where do we go from here?"

Chloe tapped her finger on her chin. "We dig. She mentioned an EMT father. She may be telling the truth about that being the source of her fascination with crime scenes. And when we asked about revenge, I got the feeling she had personal experience to draw on. Let's see if we can find friends or work acquaintances who might be able to shed some light on that."

Gabe looked up from taking notes. "And the other two?"

"Fortner is an ambulance chaser. He'd be in ninety percent of the crime-scene photos you have on file, I'd guess. The bank teller–backup singer is a possibility, but it's a stretch. Making a guess, she wants more from her life—maybe she had visions of herself as a star and the fire scenes were all the excitement she could find in this little town."

"Couldn't that translate into trying to create excitement by starting the fires or re-creating a crime that got a lot of attention?" Gabe lifted his pen from the pad.

"Good point. Yes, it could, which is why I asked your boss, Cruse Conyers, to put a tail on her. We'll interview her again, too. If we get answers that are too inconsistent, we'll know something is up.

Gabe left the room and came back with two black coffees in foam cups. "Bad coffee, but better than nothing. Who do you think we're looking for?"

She leaned back in her chair, looked into the thick black liquid. Gabe was a good cop, but more than that, an intuitive one. She owed him the truth. "It's complicated, Gabe."

He laid his pencil and pad down. "I know."

"I talked to my supervisor earlier. He doesn't necessarily agree with me on this. I want you to know that up front."

"Okay." Gabe leaned back in his chair, tipping it back on two legs.

Chloe sipped the bitter black brew. Stalling. "I think we might be looking for a woman. Some of the aspects of these crimes make me think it's possible, maybe even likely. My boss doesn't agree. Most arsonists are male, especially when murder is involved.

"I haven't got a handle on it yet, but I think this person has a very active fantasy life concerning your pastor. If you look at the women who were killed, a woman he was engaged to and one who was spreading the word that she wanted to be engaged to him. And then there's Sailor, someone Jake dated."

"Briefly," Gabe growled.

"Granted. Then you have the church. Taking him away from whoever this person is that thinks she deserves his time and attention. She might even be someone that he's counseled, someone a little unstable, but who functions pretty normally."

Gabe rubbed the stubble on his cheeks with a weary hand, then shrugged. "It makes sense to me. I still think we should keep a tail on Elaine Barbury. She seems pretty unstable."

"Agreed. Gabe, these women were a starting place, but there will be others. There's a good chance that the person who set the fire won't be in the photos at all. That he or she either watched from a safe distance or didn't watch at all. The crime scenes were so organized that I wouldn't doubt it. Can you cross-check rental properties with people in town during both murders?"

Gabe visibly swallowed a groan. "I can, but it'll take a while. A tourist town like this one has more than a few, but then you'd know that."

Chloe smiled. "Yeah."

"I'll get right on that." He let the chair drop to all four feet and pushed to a standing position.

"There's one more thing, Gabe." Chloe chewed her bottom lip and tried not to focus on the fact that she felt like she was betraying a friend. Doing her job and keeping the case on the straight-up was the best she could do for all of them. "My boss has been doing this a long time. He thinks that we should consider that it's Jake."

"What?"

"Not the original crime, but the latest ones. It could be an explanation for the long period between murders."

"It's not Jake."

"I know." She knew it with every fiber of her being. But she needed to be able to prove it.

"Do you?" His eyes challenged her.

She lifted the heavy weight of her hair off her neck and let it drop, making her shoulders relax, too. "Yes, I do know it's not Jake. He was with me before the church fire. I guess it's possible he could've set it earlier, but I don't think so. His reaction was sincere."

The phone at Gabe's hip buzzed. He looked at the number and stood. "I've got to go. I hope you know what you're doing. I've read the statistics, Chloe. I know arsonists are some of the most difficult criminals to catch, but this is more than just starting fires. This is murder. We've got to put this away. Our town can't survive months of this. Jake can't."

As he walked out the door, she grabbed her phone and the files. Did she know what she was doing? She'd survived in undercover work only because she'd learned to read people. Who was important, who worked for whom, when something big was going down. When they started suspecting her.

She prayed that she got this right. She was staking her reputation with the Serial Crimes Unit on it.

But more than important, she was staking Jake's life.

He'd been at the church all morning, working with a group of volunteers to get things ready enough to have services on Sunday. She wanted to join them.

She wasn't going to check on Jake. He was a grown man perfectly able to take care of himself.

So he had become more than the average witness to her. It was still her job to make sure that he stayed safe.

Leaning his shovel against the wall, Jake pulled off his work gloves and stretched his aching back. He would pay for the hours of shoveling soggy drywall later, but with only the muscle pain and spasms that had become a normal part of life. He'd learned to tell the difference between that kind of pain and the pain that would rob him of the ability to walk.

Doctors had warned him: no hard physical labor. The next injury could well be his last. The injury to his spine had come very close to paralyzing him, had in fact for a couple of weeks. That it had healed was a wonder no one questioned, and one he didn't take for granted.

He didn't take chances.

He knew he was blessed, despite the backbreaking work and the heartbreaking fact that his church was literally a shell of what it had once been. People had been showing up all day to help.

He'd been overwhelmed by the generosity of his community. Off-duty firefighters had been directing the work hauling debris. A group of teachers had come over to help clean up. At least twenty-five or thirty church members had taken the day off work to be here. Even Anna, the young woman he'd helped find food the other night, had shown up. She was monitoring the playground, keeping a close eye on the volunteers' kids.

A warm breeze blew in through the open window. He could hear the laughter of the women outside as they painted the furniture from the children's wing, remarkably undamaged except for smoke. He caught sight of red hair behind a woman in a maternity shirt, both of them passing out sandwiches and drinks.

Chloe and Sailor. The two had been through a lot in the not-so-distant past when a woman Sailor had loved and trusted had turned out to be a drug dealer. Sailor had barely survived. Chloe, along with Sailor's husband, Gabe, had been part of the undercover sting that brought the drug ring down.

Chloe wasn't dressed like a cop today, more like a teenager, in low-rider jeans and a long-sleeved T-shirt.

And as she moved through the group behind Sailor, she had a ready smile and kind comment. He could hear the laughter through the open window.

Bayley Conyers, the police lieutenant's wife and Sailor's sister-in-law, took a sandwich from the tray and looked up, catching Jake's eye on Chloe. She looked at Chloe and back at him, her eyebrows shooting to her hairline. Oh, yeah, that's just what he needed—one of the happily married women in the church trying to fix him up with Chloe.

Maybe it was no secret that he'd wanted to be married. He'd wanted a family. He thought at one time it would be with Julie. She was sweet and shy, pretty in an understated way. Nothing like his rebellious mother. Everything he'd thought he wanted.

And now, under his skin like a rash, was a certain strong-willed, redheaded cop. He even liked her mile-wide independent streak.

Glutton for punishment. That's all he could think. He pulled his gloves back on and hauled the tarp of debris out into the sunlight. Matt Clark met him at the door, taking the tarp to haul to the dump truck. Lara Hughes, dressed today in jeans and a T-shirt instead of her typical department gear, pressed a bottle of water into his hand.

"Thanks." He smiled at his friend, who'd never made him think thoughts of little redheaded children. For one thing, she didn't have red hair.

"It looks like things are really bad, I know, Jake, but most of this stuff is cosmetic. Drywall's cheap and you've got lots of labor."

"You're right." He stuck his gloves under one arm, glugged half the bottle of water and swiped at his mouth with the back of a grimy hand. Ugh. Should've left the gloves on.

"Chloe thinks the person who is doing all this is very likely someone we know. Someone who lives in Sea Breeze. Maybe even a friend. Do you think that's possible?"

Lara's hazel eyes narrowed on his. "Are you asking me if I think this perp could be a firefighter?"

"No." Jake turned up the palm of his hand. "Maybe. I don't know. It's possible, I guess, but we're kind of family, you know? It's hard for me to believe that one of us would hurt our own."

Lara studied the guys she worked with as they shoveled wet drywall into the back of a truck. "We've all read the statistics, Jake. The hero complex…it happens. But this—what's happened to you is something different. I'd be really shocked if it was somebody from our department."

"That's the way I feel, too. Thanks."

As she walked away, he took another big swig of water and threw the empty bottle onto a pile of trash. Somebody he knew. Even the thought of it made him sick.

Laughter across the churchyard drew his eye. Chloe and Bayley had taken over for the painting crew while they ate. Bayley Conyers, unrestrained as always, threw her head back as she laughed. Chloe, a little more self-possessed, dipped her head forward, but mirth shimmered in her eyes when she looked up at him.

"What's so funny?"

She glanced at Bayley. "My landlady here was just telling me about Palm Sunday last year when you were supposed to be playing Jesus riding in on the donkey."

He made a face. "That crazy donkey wouldn't budge. I had to get off and push from behind while Cruse pulled from the front. First Palm Sunday ever where Jesus pushed the donkey through the palms."

"Bet the kids didn't care. I bet they'll remember it for a long time." She laughed again, her hair dipping forward to brush the ends through the fresh paint on the tiny table.

"You're going to end up with more paint in your hair than on the table. Hang on a sec...." He stuck his hand in his back pocket and came up with a piece of twine.

Bayley jumped to her feet. "I've gotta run—check on—Sailor. Make sure she hasn't been on her feet too long."

Chloe reached up, pulling her hair off her neck, fumbling with it and losing it from one side and then the other as she tried not to transfer more paint from her hands to her hair. Jake tried to help gather it in, going still as his fingers touched hers, her hair smooth as silk around them.

Her hands dropped. She was so small, smaller in bare feet than he'd remembered. She always had on those high heels. He tied the string and stepped away. "You'll be a trendsetter. Before long everyone will be painting the ends of their hair purple."

As she turned to face him, she caught his eyes for a second before smirking and waving the paintbrush at him. "We can start with yours."

"I'll pass this time." He held out his hand.

She handed him Bayley's paintbrush. "You don't think she was a little obvious, do you?"

Jake stooped beside her to begin painting the child-sized table's legs. "Bayley's been trying to set me up ever since she and Cruse got together. She's one of those."

"Aah."

As the sun started to go down, the volunteers trickled away. Chloe picked up her bag. "I guess I'll head back to the house, try to get some work done."

"Thanks for helping."

"It's no big deal." She started for the car, Jake keeping pace beside her.

"It is. It's not your church or your town, but you gave your time to help out. That's pretty special in my book."

"Nobody made me feel like an outsider." Chloe stuck her hand in her jeans pocket and came up with her keys. She opened the door and stood in the gap, her fingers on the rim of the door. "That makes your church a pretty special place."

Jake placed his hands on each of hers. "Chloe, be careful. There's someone out there trying to get to people that are connected to me and this…feels like a connection. I don't want you to be hurt."

She didn't argue, just nodded. "I'll be careful. I promise." She slid into the car and closed the door.

He watched as she drove out of the parking lot. As much as he wanted to forget what had happened and trust that things would be the same around here, he couldn't. Not with the guts of his church spilled out all over the yard.

He noticed one last car in the parking lot—the young babysitter Anna's old hunk. He thought she'd left two hours ago when the last of the volunteers with young children left. He walked over to it, trying to tamp down the gut feeling that something was wrong.

Her car probably wouldn't start and she caught a ride home with someone.

But wouldn't she have let him know? The dented door groaned as he jerked it opened. When he saw the baby's diaper bag on the passenger seat, he pulled his cell phone out of his back pocket to call Gabe. He didn't know her well, but she cared for that baby's needs well before she cared for her own. There was no way she'd leave his bag.

Off-duty and home with his new wife, Gabe snarled into the phone. "Jake, this better be important."

"I've got a bad feeling. Anna Prentiss, the babysitter. Her car was left in the parking lot. I think someone might have taken her from the church. She's got an apartment over the old Franklin building. You know where I'm talking about?"

"Yes. I'll send a unit over there, but, Jake, I think you're probably overreacting."

"She's got a baby, Gabe." As he talked, Jake spotted something on the floor that made his blood turn to ice. He dug in his pocket for a tissue and gently picked it up. "You better send the fire department. I think he's got her."

Jake ran for his 4Runner, throwing the bubble light on the dash as soon as he got in. He roared out of the parking lot, a matchbook clutched in his hand.

SEVEN

Chloe got the call just as she was about to wash the purple paint out of her hair. She knew before she got to the address that it wasn't a false alarm. The now-familiar smudge of gray-black smoke in the sky warned her.

She couldn't get close to Anna's apartment because of the emergency vehicles, so she threw on an FBI windbreaker over her paint-splotched T-shirt and jeans and fought her way through the yellow tape toward the old waterfront building. She could hear Jake yelling as she got closer. And when she was close enough to see, she saw that that Captain Caruso had him cornered up against a truck.

"Stand down, Jake. You're not going in. That's my final decision."

Jake couldn't let it go. His body strained forward with every breath. "Cap, I'll stay out of the way."

"No. You'll divide their attention. And they need every bit of concentration they can muster. Who knows what kind of trap that madman might have set in there?"

"You're right, I'm sorry." Jake's shoulders sagged.

The captain walked away and Jake leaned against the truck. As she walked close, he glanced up and then down again at his feet. "I guess you heard that."

"Couldn't really help it."

"He's right. I'm out of shape. I'd only be putting them more in danger."

He wasn't out of shape. His body was as well-defined as any of those guys'. And he would put himself on the line in a second, just like they did. But his calling was different. "Jake, all of those guys—and Lara—can do the job in there. They're great at it. But you are the only one who can do the job out here. You're the only one who can stand with the victims, and for them, the way you do."

He raised his eyes to meet hers, the sadness in them making her heart hurt. She picked her words with care. "The way I see it, that makes you a necessary part of the team, not a has-been."

He scrubbed his face with his hands. "It's my fault she's in there."

She grabbed him by his turnout coat, forcing him to look at her. "*No, it's not.* It's the fault of the killer who took her and set the fire."

The door to the street kicked open wide, smoke billowing. Matt Clark burst through it with Anna in his arms. Within seconds, the EMTs were bent over her, working to open her airway, getting precious oxygen to her.

"Where's Mason? Where's the *baby?*" Jake's low groan hit Chloe like a punch in the stomach.

Matt Clark jogged back toward the house, pulling his faceshield down and settling his helmet into place. As he did, Lara came out the door, a blanket-covered bundle in her arms.

"Thank you, God," Jake breathed.

The ambulance doors slammed and the siren started its slow wail. "Why aren't they waiting for the baby?" Chloe asked.

Jake glanced back at the ambulance. "They'll have another ambulance on the way. If they were having problems resuscitating her, they would go ahead and take off like that. They're probably headed to the nearest open space to meet LifeFlight."

Sure enough, Chloe could hear the distant sound of the helicopter's rotors. As Lara got closer with the baby, she could also hear Mason screaming. *Thank God.*

The EMTs on scene checked Mason out as best they could, but they couldn't calm him down. He fought them, kicking and coughing every breath, tears streaming down his face.

Jake's fists were clenched at his sides.

Chloe gave him a little shove. "Go to him."

"They don't need my help."

"Apparently they do, since there's no way they can hear anything through that stethoscope right now."

Jake looked at Chloe. Her stance was all business, her arms crossed, her law-enforcement jacket open to show a badge and gun. And the tips of her hair were purple.

"Go to him." She smiled and he was lost.

"Okay, fine. You're right." He walked to the small group huddled around the flailing baby. The firefighters around him stepped back to let Jake in. "He okay?"

Todd, a firefighter EMT, shrugged one muscular shoulder. "As far as I can tell. Lara found him closed up in the closet. Someone obviously put him there. Some clothes were kicked up in front of the door, she said. Maybe to make it hard to find him. No clue."

"Smoke inhalation? Burns?"

The big firefighter shrugged again. "No burns. He's crying too hard to for me to get a good listen."

Jake leaned forward, put his hand on Mason's back and talked low, in the little boy's ear. "Hey, bud, remember me?"

Mason turned toward his voice, huge blue eyes full of fear and distrust, sweaty baby hair stuck to his head. When he saw Jake, he didn't hesitate, but lurched into his arms.

Jake caught him in an awkward hug. "Hey, Mason. Hey, bud, you're okay."

The baby cinched chubby arms around Jake's neck and held on tight, and as Jake rubbed circles on the tiny frame, the wails turned to sobs and finally hiccuping sighs. With one long, shuddering sigh, Mason stuffed his thumb in his mouth and closed his eyes.

Todd, the EMT, quickly stepped forward to place the stethoscope on the baby's back. Now that Mason was quiet, he could hear good breath sounds. He gave the crew standing around a thumbs-up and moved back. "I'd take him to the hospital to be checked out by the ER docs but all signs say he's in good shape."

"They were both pretty lucky that you noticed her car in the church parking lot, Jake. If we hadn't gotten the call when we did…" Lara shook her head. "I think the only reason she was alive is that the guy didn't have time to finish what he'd planned, thanks to you."

Gabe Sloan walked into their tight circle and jerked his head toward the yellow tape line where a crowd had gathered, including local news media with their lights and cameras. "Let's reserve the talk for later."

They scattered back to work, Lara and Matt and the other firefighters to the building, except for Todd, who stuck close to Mason.

Cops pulled back the yellow tape to allow the arriving ambulance into the perimeter and as Jake climbed into it with baby Mason, his eyes met Chloe's across the parking lot. She held her camera in her hands and looked grim, the way he felt.

The killer was now choosing people who had a peripheral relationship to Jake, lashing out in a vicious and frightening attack on Anna Prentiss.

If they didn't manage to stop him, who knew what innocent might be next?

Chloe focused her Nikon on the crowd and made a mental note to touch base with the camera crew from the local television station. A blurry cap in the distance came into focus as she zoomed in. Elaine Barbury. *Click.*

A tap on her shoulder startled her. She turned to see the firefighter she'd tagged as having a crush on Lara Hughes. Matt Clark?

"Are you getting close to getting this guy?" His jaw bunched.

"We're making some progress." She tilted her head,

studying him. "Do you have a personal stake in this case, Matt?"

He looked back toward the wood-and-brick apartment building. "Jake's my friend. When he had to leave the department, it was like cutting off a piece of my arm." His eyes met hers then, and the anger and hurt made her scared for him. "I want to take this guy down."

"I'll help you. When we find the person who did this, we'll put him away." She meant it as comfort, but it didn't seem to make much difference to Matt Clark.

Matt jerked his head back, macho guy equivalent of a nod. "The captain says you can come in now."

She followed him toward the old building, her heart pounding. A new crime scene meant new evidence. New pieces to tie the criminal to the crime. Even if the evidence didn't lead to the perpetrator, it would help put him or her away.

The door hung on its hinges where the firefighters had kicked it in. She walked up the stairs to the loft apartment. The stench of the extinguished fire hung in the air as Chloe stepped in, booties on her feet. She'd told Jake that fire scenes didn't bother her.

Not strictly the truth.

She didn't remember the fire that killed her parents. But images of fire stalked her sleep. And the smoke that still curled from the surfaces in this apartment gave her a tough, tight-chested minute before she could draw a deep breath. She looked around and made herself focus, not on the obvious—the fire—but what wasn't quite so obvious: the evidence. With so many emergency personnel in and out, it would be hard to isolate, but they'd still do their best to collect what they could.

In many places the studs were exposed, charred, nearly burned through in some cases. The ceiling, too. Flames had eaten through most of the ceiling in the small living room and had crawled into the bedroom overhead. The fire inspector pointed to a couple of areas where the burn pattern indicated ignition. The firefighters on scene would cut out pieces of the wall to be tagged as evidence, but along with the crime-scene investigators, she took photographs with her digital camera.

In the corner, one of the investigators was asking quiet questions of one of the firefighters while the memory was still fresh in his head: How fast did the fire take hold? Was it an odd color? Where was the hottest burn?

Gabe entered the room from the bedroom. "You'll want to take pictures in there."

Chloe stepped carefully over the threshold. The scene looked remarkably similar to the photos of Sharon Hardin and Julie Mansford's, except for one glaring difference. The big number three spray-painted over the bed. "There's the same little figurine and the silver cross."

"We haven't been able to get a lead on the figurine. The cross is sold at hundreds of retail outlets, about forty of which are within driving distance of Sea Breeze. It's a dead end for us." Gabe shoved his hands into his jeans pockets.

"And the nightgown?"

He shook his head. "Very popular online order. We're running down the credit-card charges with the company but so far we haven't had any hits that intersect with our case."

She pulled an evidence bag out of her jacket pocket. "Jake found this in Anna's car. He didn't touch the matchbook. Maybe we'll get lucky and get a print."

"And maybe it belongs to her. This is ridiculous. How can we have all this evidence and not be able to link it to any suspects?" Gabe walked out the door, pushing past one of the techs, not answering when the guy called out a question.

"The fire eats up the trace. And what the fire doesn't get, the high water pressure washes away." Maria Fuentes didn't look up from where she was pulling fibers from the bed covers with tape. "We'll try to get every impression we can from the firefighters who were first on scene, but it's understandable that he would be frustrated."

Chloe looked out the sooty window. The flashing lights of the emergency vehicles looked weird through the veil of the dirty window.

She glanced back at Maria. "Everybody says you're the best. If anyone can find the piece that'll lead us to him, it'll be you."

Maria gave an unladylike snort. "You don't have to compliment me, FBI. I know how good I am."

Chloe smiled. "Glad to hear it."

Something caught her eye just under the edge of the dust ruffle by the leg of the bed. Something small and round. "Maria, do you have tweezers?"

Maria took them out of the kit at her waist and

watched as Chloe plucked a small brass disc out of the squishy carpet. It had a hole in the top and a small indented *E* stamped on the surface. Maybe a charm of some kind.

"Look at you." Maria held out an evidence bag. "I think we may have to start what you'd call a mutual admiration society."

Chloe turned the tiny piece of jewelry, studying it closely. It didn't look remarkable, yet it could be the key to closing this case. She dropped it in the bag.

Maria closed the bag and stretched to her feet, pressing gloved fingers into the muscles in her lower back. "I'll test that charm for fingerprints and any trace. We might get lucky. It's not the usual kind of thing people would think to wipe clean."

Chloe took one last look around and barely restrained a shudder at the charred door frame to the pint-sized bathroom. Anna had been lucky to be found alive. "I'm going over to the hospital to check on Anna Prentiss. If you find anything, call my cell phone."

"We'll get this guy."

Chloe met Maria's eyes. "You can count on that. I want this unsub in jail. Yesterday."

Jake lifted a sleeping Mason from the borrowed car seat in the backseat of his 4Runner. "Bayley Conyers collected some things for Mason—pjs and a porta-crib, a few clothes. And she's offered to let Anna and Mason stay in their guest room for a while when Anna gets out of the hospital tomorrow."

"He wouldn't go to anyone else, huh?" Chloe held the door open for him.

"Nope, screamed every time I tried to detach him from my neck." Jake patted the little boy's back.

"He equates you with safety, especially with his mom not around. It's sweet." Chloe picked up a brand-new toddler-sized suitcase from the floor of the porch and laughed. "There's a ton of stuff in here. Clothes. Toys. Oh, and diapers and wipes."

"Bayley asked me if Mason was potty-trained. How'm I supposed to know that?" Jake turned the key and pushed open the door to his house. There was a light on in the kitchen and the house smelled like burned coffee.

"That's weird. I made coffee this morning, but I'm pretty sure I washed the pot out. Too many years looking after myself."

"Get Gabe on the phone." Before his eyes, Chloe morphed into cop mode, her brown eyes going hard and flat, her weapon poised to use at a moment's notice. She waved him back to the door with her left hand as she started down the hall. "Stay here."

Where would he be going with an armload of two-year-old? Tension tightened his shoulders, knowing that she was putting herself in danger as he stood waiting. All he could do was call Gabe and pray that God protected them as she cleared the rooms of his house one by one.

In the kitchen, she called out to him. "We're clear, but I need you to take a look at something."

He hitched Mason up a little higher—the kid slept like a rock—and joined her in the kitchen. His empty coffeepot, empty except for the burned dregs, sat on the side-board. Beside it, one of his coffee mugs with a perfect lipstick ring. He had to force himself to take a breath.

"Do you think the killer is a woman?" He pushed the words out between clenched teeth.

"It's a possibility we can't ignore. That the killer came here to leave you a message."

Gabe stepped through the open front door, Maria, the crime-scene investigator, right behind him.

Chloe slipped out of her FBI coat and tossed it onto a kitchen chair. "Sorry to bring you out so late. I know you came straight from the other scene. But I think we might have DNA evidence here."

Maria pulled a plastic bag out of her kit. "It's no biggie. I was just finishing up at Anna's apartment, anyway. So what do we have here?"

Gabe stooped to look at the mug on the counter. "Jake, I'd say either you have a very persistent admirer or our killer was telling you that he or she can get to you anytime. I'll have one of our patrol officers sit across the street tonight. We'll try to make more permanent arrangements tomorrow. Chloe, I think you should consider staying with me and Sailor. As much time as you're spending with Jake, you just might have a target painted on your back."

Anger and dread balled in the pit of Jake's stomach. That someone would do this, harm an innocent young woman, risk her baby, and bring a threat to Chloe, just because they'd spent time with him. Mason stirred and Jake patted him back to sleep.

As Maria brushed fingerprint dust onto the coffeepot and mug, Chloe paced. "I've got more photos of the crime scene. We'll take a look at those tomorrow, along with the rosters of the fire department and anyone who wasn't on duty this afternoon."

Jake stopped patting Mason. "This is *not* a firefighter."

"I agree, Jake, in that I don't think these crimes fit a firefighter profile, but we have to explore every angle, cross every *T.*" Chloe held the evidence bag as Maria dropped the mug in. "And thanks for the offer, Gabe, but I've been in worse situations. For now I'll keep staying at Bayley's beach house."

Emotions Jake thought he'd long buried swirled inside him. He didn't want to hear about how Chloe'd been in worse situations, even though he knew she must've been. In her undercover career, she would've come up against some pretty bad people. She looked cool and confident, the direct opposite of how he felt.

He was definitely not cool with things the way they were.

As he patted little Mason, carrying him as he checked things out around his condo, Chloe brought the porta-crib in from the front porch and began to put it up in Jake's room, muttering something about engineering degrees.

It wasn't the first time his world had been rocked off its predictable little axis, but he'd sure hoped Julie's death would be the last time he faced such a cataclysmic event. He had to admit that maybe one reason he hadn't found anyone he wanted to date had more to do with him not wanting to risk loving again than the fact that the women weren't right for him.

And now was a great time to realize that it didn't seem to matter that he'd been protecting himself. The killer still had the ability to get to people he cared about.

Chloe dropped the mattress into the crib with a plop. "There. All ready for the little man. If he'll let you put him down."

"He's pretty tired. I think he'll sleep straight through it." Gently, Jake laid the baby down on his back. Mason sighed and hitched over onto his side, popping his thumb in his mouth and sucking a few times before letting it fall out of his mouth completely.

"Nice job." Chloe smiled.

He found himself smiling back. "You did good with the crib. No advance degree necessary?"

"It was touch and go for a while," she whispered.

They stood each on one side of the crib, staring at each other until Maria broke up the moment. "Hey, sport, I'm heading out. Gabe's already gone to make arrangements for a detail outside your house tonight." She looked from one to the other. "Okay, then. See ya. Don't bother seeing me out. I'll lock up."

Neither one moved as they stood over Mason's crib. Finally, Chloe reached for a blanket from the bag Bayley had collected and covered the toddler.

"Do you want me and my gun to stay tonight?" She followed him out of the room, halfway holding her breath.

Jake walked into the kitchen, stretching his back that had kinked up as he held the baby. "Yes. But that's the last thing either one of us needs. No matter how innocent, the whole town would be talking in the amount of time it took Mrs. Walchowski across the street to get her newspaper off the front porch and put her coffee cup down to pick up the phone."

A wisp of a smile lifted the corners of her mouth. "She sounds like someone I should recruit for the FBI."

He shuddered. "She's too tough for the FBI. Believe me."

She laughed, but her expression turned serious. "It's going to make him—or her—mad that he missed today. Please be careful. Be aware of your surroundings at all times."

"I will. I am. You take care of you, too."

She reached for the doorknob and he grabbed her hand without thinking, pulling her close. She sighed, a sweet sound, unlike any he'd heard from the very independent, very put-together Ms. Davis. With hands as soft as he could make them, he cupped her face, sliding his fingers into the silk of her fine red hair, smiling again when he felt the paint at the tips.

Leaning forward, he brushed her lips with his, just a whisper of a touch, before he let her go.

He opened the door for her. "I mean it, Chloe. I don't want another person I care about to get hurt."

EIGHT

On her third cup of coffee by ten in the morning, Chloe tossed the new photos onto the kitchen table. The bright spring sunlight poured through the windows, warming her back, making her blink sleepily. She hadn't slept well, thinking about Jake alone in his condo watching over a little baby who had very nearly died yesterday.

She didn't want to think about the kiss. The very same kiss that had her long-dormant hormones sounding trumpets and throwing ticker-tape parades at just the thought after so many years undercover. It was a little hard to date when no one knew your real name. And now…now she needed to focus on her career.

Right. Focus. She needed to give her happy-dancing hormones a reality check and move on.

The video footage that she'd commandeered from the television crews after she left Jake's house last night didn't reveal anything new. The backup singer had been cleared. Cops were shadowing her when the attempted murder took place. She'd been shoe shopping an hour away at the outlet mall. If a better alibi existed than a police surveil-lance team, Chloe didn't know what it would be.

Elaine Barbury couldn't be cleared, but Chloe's gut told her Elaine wasn't the one behind this. She had some of the markers but not all. Something definitely wasn't right about Elaine, but serial killer? It didn't fit.

The sound of tires on the shell driveway outside had her peeking out the window to see a red 4Runner. Jake?

She met him at the back door that led to the deck. "Hey, what's up? Where's your little sidekick this morning?"

"With his mom and very relieved to be there. Appar-ently Cap'n Crunch is not the breakfast of champions when you're two. He wanted pancakes and I didn't have any, which led to a full-out tantrum." Jake's eyes were big, vibrant blue.

"Cute."

"Not so cute when you have Cap'n Crunch all over your kitchen."

"What'd you do?" She took a grocery bag from him and held the door open with the other hand.

He shot a look at her. "I took him to the diner for pancakes, of course. No telling what might've happened to my house if I hadn't."

"How's his mom doing?"

"She's hanging in there. Happy to be alive. Scared that the killer could get to her so easily." He walked into the kitchen, painted the color of orange juice.

"I'll give her some time to recover and then I'd like to talk to her." She plunked the bag on the counter.

"According to Gabe, she doesn't remember anything

after going to her car." He placed the other bags on the counter and started taking stuff out. Flour, butter, eggs, sugar. Chocolate chips?

"Jake, what is all this stuff?"

"I noticed your candles."

Confusion drew her brows together. What did candles and baking supplies have to do with each other? "And?"

"They smell really good, but they don't begin to compare to the real thing."

"And you know this how?"

"My grandma." When his eyes found hers, they were sad. "After my dad died, my mom lost it. The three of us hadn't lived together for a long time, but I think she always hoped…"

He cleared his throat. "She sent me to live with my grandmother. And I felt like I lost my mom and my dad all at the same time. For a while, I really hated my mom for taking my family away from me."

Chloe lined up the supplies on the counter. "I can understand that."

He moved some around to put them in order. "Every afternoon after school when I would come in, my grandmother would have the supplies lined up like this out on the table. She would make me stir while she measured the ingredients and poured them in. At first she did all the talking…but eventually, I started telling her about my day at school. And finally, I talked to her about my parents. She taught me how to forgive them."

Tears clogged Chloe's throat, her heart so full she

couldn't breathe, and she couldn't even say why. "Didn't you feel abandoned?"

"Yeah." Without looking at her, he handed her a spoon and started measuring sugar into the mixing bowl with two sticks of soft butter. "Stir."

He took one look at her face as she stood there not moving and chuckled. Taking the spoon, he said, "Like this."

He creamed the butter into the sugar, his biceps bulging against the brushed cotton of his T-shirt. She forced her eyes back to the bowl.

The silence stretched between them. Chloe took the spoon back, scraping the edge of the bowl as Jake began to crack eggs. "I remember what having parents was like. My mother would sit at the table doing puzzles with me. Our favorite thing was lying in grass in the front yard looking at the sky for hours, talking about the clouds. My daddy would come home from work and point out places on the map that we would visit one day. I was almost six when they died.

"Still a baby, really." She whipped the butter and sugar together like she'd seen Jake do, until it was soft and creamy. "And when they were gone, no one wanted a precocious little girl who'd been brought up to ask too many questions."

"Taste that."

She darted a look at his face. He was serious. She licked a tiny taste off the end of the wooden spoon. The brown sugar gave the butter a caramel taste. She closed her eyes, smiled. "Mmm, really good."

"Just wait." He took the dry ingredients and measured them into a bowl. "I know what it feels like to be unwanted, Chloe."

Her chest burned and though words crowded in her throat, she couldn't talk.

He began sifting the dry ingredients together. "My grandma told me that my life was like all these little ingredients. Life was stirring them up. It was up to me to figure out the recipe for something good or to leave something out and make really bad cookies."

She snorted a laugh then. "It appears you made some really good cookies with your life."

"That wasn't always the case—because I was convinced that I wasn't worth it. My dad obviously didn't care about me enough to stick around. After he died, my mother didn't want me. So for a while, I did just about every self-destructive thing I could think of, trying to get my grandmother to prove she didn't love me, either. I never missed an afternoon baking cookies, though. Here, put the eggs in and then we'll put the dry mixture in with the wet."

She poured the eggs in and began to cautiously scrape the spoon around the edge of the bowl. "Like this?"

"No, don't be so timid. You're being too careful with it. Make a little mess. We'll clean it up later." He began to really stir the mix, sloshing flour out onto the counter.

She laughed again. "*You'll* clean it up later. One thing I did learn at all those foster homes is 'you mess it up, you clean it up.'"

"Good rule." As the dough stiffened, he began to turn it more slowly in the bowl.

Jake may have felt unlovable and unloved, but Chloe had *been* unloved. The foster families, her relatives— all of them had made that clear. It was only later, when she'd found the FBI, that she'd found a place to belong. The very thing that had made her an outcast as a kid— her intellect—was what made her appealing to the FBI, but even then she'd been on her own.

The thing she wanted to know most was how did Jake become the man who loved people and trusted God, even after all that? Even now? "So, what happened? Did your grandmother send you away?"

"No, despite everything, she kept bringing me closer. I'm convinced it was only the Lord that gave her the power to love me as a rebellious teenage boy. So one day, while we were baking cookies, she laid it on the line. She said she knew I'd been hurt, but sorta like the cookies, it was only by going through the heat that we found out who God truly meant for us to be. A bunch of ingredients mixed together…or a truly fabulous chocolate-chip cookie."

She looked at him, her eyes stinging with unshed tears. "Why are you telling me this?"

"I wanted you to know I think you're a pretty great cookie." His smile tilted the corner of his lips up and made the dimple in his cheek deepen. "You've been through some heat, Chloe. I know you have. But I want you to know that you are loved by God. And you have friends here."

She pressed her lips together, willing herself not to cry. "So can we get this bunch of ingredients in the oven or are we going to talk all day?"

Jake didn't push her. He didn't even look disappointed. He picked up a spoon and started scooping the dough onto a cookie sheet.

It wasn't until hours later when she came back to the house after interviewing Anna Prentiss that she realized…Jake had made this empty rental house feel and smell like a home. It made her want something she hadn't wanted in a long, long time. And it terrified her.

The longer she stayed here, the more attached she got to this town and the people who lived here, not to mention a certain kindhearted, ruggedly handsome pastor. The problem was she knew from experience that the more you cared, the harder it was to say goodbye. Putting down roots wasn't for her. She was good at her job. She wasn't good at building relationships. She was good at moving on. And whether they caught this guy or not, that was exactly what she'd be doing in a few days.

The smoky smell lingered, but in the newly painted office suite, Jake could nearly convince himself that a fire hadn't nearly taken his church building away from him. Just like he'd nearly managed to convince himself that kissing Chloe had been an anomaly. It had been an emotional day—he'd been worried and afraid. He also managed to bake cookies with her this morning without kissing her again. So why did he feel so torn up inside?

He walked to the bookshelf and straightened the framed copy of the firefighter chaplain's prayer, wishing he could straighten his life as easily. He wanted to be with Chloe. Weird, wasn't it, that he'd spent this time searching for someone right for him and he'd stumbled upon Chloe and she just somehow fit?

A brisk knock at the open door of his office brought him back to his present surroundings. His assistant, Susan Paulson, entered with a cup of coffee from Sailor Sloan's shop. "Pastor's Special, one sugar, no cream. And I made you some blueberry muffins last night. I figured you might've had a hard night after everything that happened. I know they're your favorite, and I threw in some oatmeal to make them a teensy bit healthier."

"Thanks for trying to keep me on the straight and narrow, Suse." He lifted the lid off the coffee and took a long drink.

"I always try to take care of you, Jake. That's my job." His girly-girl assistant chipped at the red paint on her thumbnail as she lingered in the door.

"Unfortunately, it's a little late today. I've already had my allotment of calories, probably for the month. I taught Chloe how to make chocolate-chip cookies this morning." He picked up scads of envelopes that had been piling up on his desk and tried to stack them in some kind of order.

"Chloe?"

He looked up at Susan, still standing in the door. "The special agent the FBI sent over? You've probably seen her around here."

"Oh, that's right. Well, I can put these out in the break room. I'm sure someone will eat them." She crossed to his desk, put the plate of muffins on one of his chairs and began helping him with the papers.

"You know, the youth ministry staff are always hungry."

Susan laughed. "You've got that straight. Can I get anything else for you?"

He grimaced at the stacks of papers. "Nope, I'm all good. Thanks for the coffee. After a night with a two-year-old, I need it. Especially if I'm going to face the paperwork that ate Detroit."

Her smile was really pretty, but it didn't reach her eyes. "Jake, can I be honest with you?"

"Of course."

She eased into the chair, sliding the muffins onto her lap. "I'm worried about you. That you're getting distracted by all that's going on. Maybe your priorities are getting a little skewed. I just—well, I'm worried is all."

Jake couldn't help but try to take the words to heart. Of all the people in the church she probably knew him best. And if she thought he couldn't handle what was going on and still do a good job as pastor, then there were a lot of other people who thought the same thing.

He considered his words carefully before he spoke. "I'm trying really hard not to let anything fall through the cracks, but with the church building the way it is, we're working under pretty tough conditions these days. Things aren't going to be normal, not for a while. Maybe not for a long while."

Her fingers were white as they gripped the edge of the plate of muffins. "I know, Jake. I just want you to know that people are watching you, waiting to see how you handle this threat against you. I really want you to succeed and get through this without any lingering doubts about you."

"Do you think people want me to leave the church?" He'd be lying if he said it hadn't crossed his mind before, but the thought of leaving the place he felt most at home, the place he felt called to serve, made him feel sick. Someone wanted to take that away from him and be happy that Jake had suffered a loss.

God, it's Your church, not mine. He took a deep breath. "If people don't feel safe, I'll leave. Maybe I should've taken a leave of absence from the beginning."

Susan grabbed for his hands. "Jake, you know that's not what people want. It's definitely not what I want. I just want you to know that some people are talking." She hesitated. "Maybe it would be best for you to steer clear of entanglements, just for a while."

"Like Chloe?"

"Yes." She nodded, but then looked unsure.

"Chloe isn't an entanglement. She's a person who's looking to find her way just like anyone else here." When Susan started to speak, he held up his hand. "But I get your point, and I'll do everything I can to keep people from thinking the worst."

"I know you will. And Chloe is welcome here, of course." She sniffed and grabbed a tissue from the stash on the corner of his desk, dabbing at her eyes.

"Hey, Suse, it's okay. All this will be over soon and we'll be back to the way things were. Maybe a little older and wiser."

She turned toward him, her pretty gray-blue eyes swimming in tears. "I know God has a plan for us, Jake."

"He does. Our church will come out of this just fine. You watch and see."

She bit hard on her lip, but no longer fought the tears.

He studied her face. She'd been dealing with a lot since all this started. "Are you all right now? Do you want to take the rest of the afternoon off?"

"Maybe I will leave a little early, get a pedicure or something. Apparently I could use a little relaxation."

He grinned at her. She'd been his assistant for the three years he'd been here, and he'd never met a woman more into that girly stuff. If she needed the afternoon off, he'd rather give it to her now than lose more days to stress and frustration.

"I'll see you tomorrow. Thanks for the coffee."

"Anytime."

As she walked out the door, he called after her. "And hey, do you mind leaving those muffins where I can find them?"

Her laugh echoed back. "Sure thing, boss."

Jake picked up the mail and sliced into the first envelope. At least twenty photos slid out onto the desk. At first he thought they were more crime-scene photos, but they weren't. They were pictures of him with Chloe. And in every photo, Chloe's face was marked out with a permanent-markered black *X*.

He threw them on the desk as if they were on fire. He'd left Chloe alone. Picking up the phone, he dialed her cell number. "Pick up. Pick up, pick up, pick up."

When her voice mail answered, he left a brief message. "Chloe, call me. It's important."

He dialed Gabe, the phone clenched in his fingers. "Have you seen Chloe?"

"Mmm, I guess. About an hour ago. Why?"

Quickly, Jake described the photos, dread balling in his stomach as he looked at them again.

"I'll send Maria Fuentes over for them. Don't touch them any more than you already have. And I'll send someone out to look for Chloe, but I'm sure she's fine. Don't worry."

Don't worry. That's what Gabe had said about Anna Prentiss right up until the time they'd seen smoke pouring out of her apartment.

Chloe leveled her stance, breathed out and squeezed the trigger. Once. Twice. Until she emptied the magazine into the target. When the range master rolled the tattered paper toward her, she could see every shot grouped where she wanted it to be.

It was one of those things that, if you didn't practice often, you lost your skill. There was a fine edge between good and great, and that tiny margin could mean the difference between life and death in the field.

She took off her ear protectors and hung them on the post beside her lane. "Thanks, Randy."

"No problem, Chloe. You'll be back tomorrow?"

She'd gotten to know her favorite former Navy SEAL when she'd been here before, so when she'd called for an appointment he'd cleared time in his schedule for her.

"If I possibly can." She pulled the rubber band out of her hair and shook it out. "Hopefully we'll catch this guy and I'll be back on the range at Quantico by week's end."

The statement gave her a twinge of loss. She would be sad to leave here, a fact that came as a huge surprise. Sea Breeze with all its small-town ways and Old South charm had managed to get under her skin. Or maybe it was just the one handsome pastor. And that was a thought she definitely didn't want to explore.

Randy scrubbed a hand over the steely gray military-short hair. "You know we'll miss you."

As she approached the locker where she'd left her stuff, she could already hear her cell phone ringing. Never a good sign. She pulled the locker open and grabbed her phone. "Chloe Davis."

"Chloe." Jake's voice, rich and a little gravelly from years of breathing smoke, held a sigh of relief.

"Hey. What's wrong?" She reached into the locker, dug her keys out of her purse.

"Where are you?"

Chloe put her bag over her shoulder, managing a wave for the girl behind the desk—a young woman who couldn't be more than nineteen, but had a nine millimeter in a holster on her hip and looked like she knew how to use it.

Outside, Chloe stopped on the sidewalk, glancing left and right to make sure she was alone. "Jake, what's this about?"

"I got some threatening pictures in the mail."

Her heart picked up speed. His tone told her it was

serious. "I can be at the church in about twenty minutes. I'm at the range."

"Can you wait there for me?" She could hear his truck pinging as he opened the driver-side door.

"No, I was leaving anyway. It'll be just as fast for me to come to you." Over the cell phone, she heard the 4Runner start up with a roar and his siren wind up. What was he doing? "Jake, what was in those pictures that could be that scary?"

"They weren't threatening *me*. You were the target. Hang on." His motor gunned and he came back on the line. "Can you just stay put until I get there?"

Perfectly capable of taking care of herself, Chloe's back went stiff. She understood that Jake felt responsible for what happened to the women in his life, so maybe she could cut him a little slack. "Okay, I'll wait here. Just hurry."

He grunted a man-response that sounded a little like "Whatever" and meant "I'm hurrying as fast as I can so get off my case."

She laughed. "I'll see you in a minute."

Chloe flipped her phone shut. He was hard-wired to be a protector. After seven years as a firefighter, it was in his blood, so not being able to save his fiancée or the woman from his church had to be eating him up. That he'd come close to losing Anna Prentiss and her baby had sent his already-protective nature into overdrive.

But just because she understood it didn't mean she had to like it. She looked around. Twenty minutes outside of town, the indoor range was a metal building that looked like a warehouse. Good security was one plus here. The lot was video monitored and her car was directly in the line of sight of the front door. The front gate would only be opened for someone who was expected. Obviously, it would still be possible to get to her here, but extremely unlikely.

Speaking of security, she needed to alert the staff that Jake was on his way. Reentering the building, she realized the young woman who'd been working the desk wasn't at her post. Chloe pulled her weapon from the holster at her lower back, leaving the safety on and carrying it at her side for now.

She cleared the hallway and the office. The building, full of staff a few minutes ago, was deserted, the hall dark and eerily quiet. She tested the door to the range, where she'd been shooting moments before. Locked tight. Continuing around the corner, she saw the exit to the outdoor shooting range sitting cracked open.

Outside, the smell of smoke drew her to the back of the building. The end of the shooting range where the targets were set up still smoldered under a coating of white foam. Range-master Randy Keane held a large fire extinguisher while several employees stomped on embers that had flown to other areas of the large field.

Randy caught sight of her standing by the door and walked toward her. "I thought you left a while ago."

"I did, but I got a call so I was waiting here for a friend. Do you know what happened?" She slid her sunglasses on against the late-afternoon glare.

"It looks like it was deliberately set. I don't have any idea who would want to set my field on fire, though."

"That call—there were some threats made against me. Do you think…"

Randy sent a hard look her way, his hand resting on his sidearm. "Are you thinking maybe it was a tactical diversion?"

She lifted a shoulder. "Maybe it was a distraction to get you to leave the front of the property open and vulnerable."

"I need to check it out."

"I'm right with you." She wasn't surprised to find the range building still empty, but a buzzer at the front desk signaled that Jake was waiting. She checked the video feed to be sure before nodding at Randy to let Jake in.

Within seconds, Jake slammed through the front door of the building. "Chloe, are you all right?"

Out of the corner of her eye, Chloe caught Randy sliding into the office to view the video monitors. "I'm fine. I was safe the whole time."

"I saw the smoke and I thought…" He almost reached for her, but didn't, instead choosing to scrub a hand through his already every-which-way, curly brown hair. "I thought that he'd gotten to you first."

His heart was so big and so troubled. She didn't think, just wrapped her arms around him. He hesitated, then drew her in close, holding her against his broad chest.

NINE

Jake buried his face in Chloe's hair, holding her close, breathing in the sweet vanilla scent, uniquely Chloe. After a long moment, he managed to drop his arms and step away. "When I saw those pictures and realized that this maniac could be coming after you, I lost it. After seeing what happened to Anna… Chloe, this person, whoever it is, isn't going to stop." He paced across the room and wheeled back to face her. "I shouldn't even be near you now."

The corners of her mouth tilted up, just a hint of a smile. "I've been taking care of myself for a long time now. Maybe it's not fair, but that's the way it is. I'm not afraid, Jake. But I am on your side. We'll find out who is doing this to you, and we will stop them."

"I forget just how fierce you are, Davis."

She tagged him with a fake punch in the arm. "You wouldn't be the first to underestimate me. It's one of my gifts, to appear young and sweet. I have to remember to take advantage of it while it lasts."

Randy poked his head out the door from the monitoring room. "Hey, Jake. I think you guys might want to see this."

The three of them squeezed into the tiny room where monitors lined the walls. Randy pointed at the screen on the far right. "I've got video coverage pretty much over the whole property. You can see here that this is the camera at the back corner of the outdoor range. I've rewound the recording to the place just before the fire starts. See, we've got nothing…nothing, and then there's a flash of black to the right. You can see a plume of fire on this monitor and a small explosion where the fire starts a few seconds later in the dry grass at the farthest corner there."

Jake stepped back at the huge burst of fire. "Whoa."

"Yeah. That's some pretty powerful stuff. It looks like our guy used some kind of incendiary round to shoot at a flammable canister. Somebody must've put it there either during an earlier visit to the range or rolled it out there just before he shot. Doesn't take a brainiac to come up with that, but it's effective."

Chloe narrowed her eyes at the screen. "Fast-forward a few frames. See that? There's another little scrap of black like the suspect is on the move after she triggers the explosions on the range. You have video coverage of the front parking lot?"

"Yes, there." Randy pointed to a screen in the middle of the bottom row. "Let me run it back to the time stamp just after what we suspect is the suspect moving away from the scene, and…"

What she saw was a blurry figure looking left and

right before rolling under the bar that restricted free entrance to the parking lot.

"Son of a gun. It *was* a diversion." Randy zoomed in to look, but the image got blurrier, so he widened the frame again. "We're not going to be able to see the face. This type of system is really so we can keep an eye on the property and take care of any problems that come up before they go nuclear, so to speak."

"If it's a digital system, we can enhance the video. Can you make me a copy?" Chloe leaned forward over Randy's shoulder. "What's he doing now?"

"I don't know—let's see if we caught it with the other camera." Randy's fingers flew on the keys.

The picture on the other monitor went black and then came into focus as their suspect panned the parking lot, took something out of a backpack and lithely rolled under Chloe's car.

Chloe's shoulders tensed. "It's a woman. She's got her hair covered, but look at how she moves, and the line of the neck. That is definitely a female."

She pushed past Jake. Or tried. He grabbed her arm. "Wait, Chloe. You don't know what she put under there or where she's watching from now. She could blow the car with you right next to it. Let me call the bomb squad."

"I've got it. My cell phone's in my bag." Pushing past him, she threw open the door into the reception area.

"I know how she feels. There's nothing worse for an operative than feeling like your hands are tied." Randy hit Enter and pushed away from the screens.

"Yeah, I can understand that." Jake knew the feeling

of wanting to take action so badly that it tasted bitter on his tongue. Knew it better than anyone could imagine. "Thanks for the help, Randy."

Outside, sirens signaled the first of the fire trucks rolling in. The cops, Joe Sheehan, silver-tinted aviators firmly in place, and Gabe Sloan, were right behind them.

Jake's phone rang. He opened it and before he could say hello, Gabe said, "What's going on, Jake? Chloe called the bomb squad?"

"We've got video of a woman planting something under Chloe's car. There's no way to know what it is, but from my training, I'd say it looked like a block of plastic explosives. Emphasis on *looked like.*"

Gabe muttered something harsh and indistinguishable over the phone line. Through the glass door, Jake could see him relaying the information to Joe Sheehan, who remained unperturbed, propped against the squad car, big arms crossed.

"All right, let's get that place evacuated."

Jake swallowed hard. "Gabe, I'm not sure that's a good idea. On the video, the woman had a weapon. If her attempt to blow Chloe up failed, she may be desperate enough to fire into the crowd."

Gabe's voice came back at him seconds later, tension vibrating in every syllable. "All right, listen, the bomb squad is ten minutes out. I'll call you back. Meantime, find Randy Keane and move the staff into the farthest room in the building away from that car."

"Got it." He flipped his phone closed as Chloe

came out from the video surveillance room with the disc in her hand.

"Here's the copy of the video. We need to get this to Maria Fuentes."

"We've got to figure a way out of here first. And after this is over, I have a feeling Maria is going to be buried in evidence for her team to process." The few staff had started to bunch up in the reception area to watch, so Jake explained the situation and recommended they leave the area for a safer place.

Randy came into the room from surveillance, shaking his head. "I don't see her if she's out there now, but the cameras are static. I can't move them unless I move them manually and there are blind spots outside the range of the cameras as we saw before."

Chloe nodded. "I understand. Can we gather your staff into a safe room?"

As Randy shooed the couple of stragglers still in the lobby down the hall, Chloe plastered herself against the glass door, trying to see what was going on outside.

"That may be bullet-resistant glass, but it's not going to stop a bomb. We need to go with them." Jake reached for her hand.

When she turned to face him, her lips were a thin, hard line. "I'm angry, Jake. Really angry."

He drew her away from the glass doors. "I'm so sorry."

"Oh, no. The responsibility for all of this lies with the crazy woman who thinks that setting these fires is the right thing to do."

He didn't say anything, just looked into her warm

brown eyes, crystal clear and full of determination. Because what he knew in his mind and what he felt in his heart were two different things. If Julie hadn't been dating him, she wouldn't have died. If Sharon Hardin hadn't tried so desperately to find a connection to him, she might still be alive, as well. How could he not feel responsible?

Randy Keane beckoned from down the hall. "Nothing in this building is really what you would call hardened against an attack of this kind, but an interior room with four walls should be safer. This is the only one left."

He shoved the two of them into a supply closet and closed the door.

In the near darkness, Chloe stared at the closed door. "Well."

Jake chuckled. "Randy's a good guy, if a little intense."

"Yeah, I get that."

He leaned against the back wall and slid until he was seated on the floor. "C'mere."

Taking one last longing look at the door, Chloe joined him on the floor. In such close quarters, she had to sit in the crook of his arm for them both to fit. He pulled her closer.

"What do you say we make us a batch of snickerdoodles when we get out of here?"

"What is that?"

"Oh, your education is sadly lacking." He thumped her gently on the head. "My grandmother didn't make only chocolate chip, she made the best snickerdoodles in the world. They're sort of like sugar cookies, but crispier, and rolled in cinnamon and sugar before they're baked."

His mouth started to water just thinking about it.

"Your grandmother made cookies with you *every* afternoon?"

"Yep."

"That's a lot of cookies."

Memories of his grandmother's kitchen threatened to overwhelm him in this dark little closet—the warmth from the oven and the late-afternoon sun streaming through the window over the sink, the aroma of the cookies baking, the time spent elbow to elbow with her. "I found out later she took them to the shut-ins in the neighborhood every morning. Back then, I just thought we ate a lot of cookies."

"There's a lot of her in you."

He had to clear his throat before he could speak. "I'm not sure that's a compliment to my grandma."

"I meant it as one." He could almost hear the grin spread across her face. "But now you don't have to make your own cookies. You have all the women in the church to bake them for you."

She was only teasing, but what she said came awfully close to what a lot of people saw in him and was pretty far from how he actually felt. "I'm not gonna lie to you, Chloe, living that bachelor lifestyle has been fun at times. But I'm tired of everyone seeing me as someone who isn't complete without his other half. I'm pretty sure that the perks of being a bachelor are no substitute for a real relationship, for having someone to come home to at night, someone who actually cares what your next thought is, and whether you're happy or not."

She sat quietly for a moment, twisting a lock of her hair with the fingers of her left hand. "I'm sorry, Jake. I wasn't thinking."

"After my crazy life growing up, I want to be married and make it last." He spoke quietly, but firmly. Not whispering a question, stating a fact.

"Losing Julie must've been a horrible blow."

He shifted. Restless in the tiny room and with the waiting, he wanted to pace, but there was no space between the shelves and the door. Instead he chose to tell the truth. "It was. That's not a lie. But we had called off the wedding."

She whipped around to look at him. "What?"

"I'm not sure who realized it first, or even who said it first, but we realized that we loved each other. We were friends—best friends. But we didn't have the feelings for each other that people have when they're in love."

"You didn't tell anyone this?"

"No." He pulled his knee up and propped his elbow on it, dropping his head on his hand. "I was in and out of consciousness for days. When I finally came around, it was all over. Julie was gone and it just didn't seem like there was any need—I didn't want people speculating about her. And my heart was broken, because I'd lost my best friend."

He looked at Chloe then. In the dim light, he could see her dark eyes, full of tears. "Hey, it's okay. It's been a long time. All this has just brought back old feelings and made me take a look at my life now and what I'm missing."

Her sharp intake of breath belied her stillness. "What are you missing, Jake?"

He laced his fingers with hers. "A partner. Someone who meets me on every level. Who isn't afraid to take me on if she thinks I'm wrong and who isn't afraid to be herself."

Chloe bit her lip. Jake held his breath as the silence stretched. He didn't know what he wanted to accomplish with this conversation. Not having planned to say any of the things that had come pouring out of his mouth, he considered that maybe he should learn some discretion.

She blew a breath out. "I think I gave up on dreams like that a long time ago. You know, most little girls grow up thinking they're a princess because they're treated like one. Mostly I just learned it was better not to have any expectations about anything except for myself. Things hurt less that way."

"Oh, Chloe." In the narrow closet, he drew her closer.

"I never really expected a hero on a white horse to come along and sweep me off my feet, Jake."

"Maybe you should."

She snorted a laugh. "Not likely now. I'm too ornery and set in my ways."

"You're worthy of being loved, Chloe." He said it matter-of-factly, like he would say the sky is blue. He meant it. "Not just because you're beautiful, but because you are who God made you to be."

She flushed a deep pink, the color warring with her red hair, even in the relative darkness. "Jake, I…"

The door slammed open. Gabe Sloan stood in the open space. "We're clear. The bomb squad defused the bomb. It didn't just look like C-4, it *was* C-4. It had a lousy detonator, but it would've done the job. The good news is that we'll have lots more evidence to follow. Your car is on its way to the precinct to be gone over with Fuentes's fine-tooth comb."

He reached a hand down and pulled Chloe to her feet. "You were lucky today. If Jake hadn't opened those pictures and shouted out the warning, you might've gotten in the car to drive away. Come on, I want to talk to you a minute and then we'll get you home."

She looked back over her shoulder as Gabe drew her out the door. Her eyes were full of something, but Jake wasn't sure what. He had a habit of saying things that maybe others wouldn't say. But he'd lost someone too soon, and there were things that hadn't been said. He didn't want to ever have that kind of regret again.

Unfortunately that meant Chloe might walk away and never look back.

TEN

Chloe's hands were cold with nerves. A room full of Sea Breeze Police officers stared at her, some with interest, some with admiration, some with downright suspicion. She had on her most professional power suit and her best shoes.

The fact that their commanding officer, Cruse Conyers, stood beside her kept the speculation to a minimum, but she had no doubt when she opened the floor to questions that they would let her have it, boss or no boss. There was a long history of mistrust between local law enforcement and the FBI, mainly because their goals were sometimes at odds.

Lieutenant Conyers cleared his throat. "Most of you have met Supervisory Special Agent Chloe Davis from the Serial Crimes Unit in the FBI. She's here to talk to us about the serial arsonist that we believe we're looking for."

She shifted the folder in her hand, wishing instead that she had a cup of Jake's Blue Mountain blend coffee to warm them. As Cruse gestured, giving her the floor, she stepped forward. "Good morning. Thank you for letting me speak to you today. I promise I'll be brief. You may already know the individual we're dealing with has already killed twice that we know of, and has attempted a third. We're also attributing various fires around town to this person, though the M.O. on those fires is different."

While speaking, she stuck the most dramatic photos of each fire that she could find to the whiteboard. Most of the cops had been on one or the other of the scenes, but seeing the images would strike at the core of their fears and drive them to do everything possible to take down this killer.

The final picture she placed on the board was a blurry shot of the unsub at the shooting range. "Our unknown subject is female, approximately twenty-eight to thirty-five years old. She has a background of abuse and probably military training of some kind. She has above-average intelligence. It would be a mistake to underestimate her, even if she appears to be nonthreatening. You should consider this person armed and dangerous."

The cops who had listened intently to her first sentence or two had begun to shift restlessly as she tagged their killer as female. One raised his hand. "You really think that this person is a woman, even though most arsonists are male?"

Chloe didn't need to check her notes for this question. "You're right that only about ten percent of arsonists are female. There's some evidence that, all along, has pointed to this being a female killer, particularly the revenge aspect of the crimes. In addition, we have video of this woman planting a bomb. The same woman was seen moments earlier shooting incendiary rounds at fuel canisters. So the answer is yes, to both your spoken and unspoken question. She is female, probably no older than thirty-four or thirty-five. And with her knowledge of firearms, she is dangerous."

She picked up her file folder. "If you have any other questions or if you find something, please call me. My business card is available here and at the front desk. By working together, we can take this killer off the streets that much faster. Thanks for your time."

She turned to Cruse. "Let's talk in your office for a minute."

He followed her in and closed the door. "Is something wrong?"

"No. But I didn't tell them everything. Organized arsonists usually tend to kill the same way, because it works for them. The person who killed Jake's fiancée and Sharon Hardin is extremely organized."

Cruse Conyers sat in his desk chair and lifted one ankle to cross over the other knee, leaning back. "Is it possible that the unsub uses two different methods based on his objective?"

"It's possible, I guess. It's very difficult to profile an arsonist because the motivations vary so widely depending on the age of the offender and the lack of evidence. There are some similarities, like the ones I mentioned. Low self-esteem, a miserable, possibly abusive childhood. Watching the tape, I'd guess that controlling the explosion makes our perp feel powerful. The murders are so different, almost ritualistic." She shook her head.

Desk chair squeaking as he moved forward, the lieutenant picked up a pencil. "Gabe Sloan seems to think you're doing fine. You held your own with the officers in there and gave them the heads-up, which is what we needed you to do. Hopefully we'll have usable video soon."

Definitely feeling dismissed, Chloe turned toward the door, but looked back. "Just out of curiosity, what did you think when Gabe Sloan recommended bringing me in for a consult?"

The lead cop didn't hesitate. "I thought we could handle it on our own. I still do. Not because I don't think you're doing a great job working with Gabe—you are—but because nine times out of ten, especially in a small community like this one, bringing in the FBI only escalates things. I think that's what happened when Anna Prentiss was attacked. And you. For whatever reason, the perp sees the FBI as a worthy adversary and it ups the ante."

"Fair enough." Though his position on things didn't agree with hers, she was professional enough to accept it without argument. Opening the door, she stepped through it before he called her name again. "Yes?"

"If this woman—whoever she is—was willing to go to the lengths she did at the shooting range...I'm not sure she's going to be willing to accept failure."

"I think Gabe has me on guard duty over Jake today."

Cruse Conyers snorted. "That should go over well."

"He's handled things better than I would if I was the target of a serial killer's game."

"Both of you need to be careful. All signs point to this being one very angry, vengeful woman." The lieutenant's phone rang. "I'll catch you later. Keep me in the loop."

Chloe thought about Cruse's words as she took the stairs down to the front door. The woman in the video didn't act like an out-of-control revenge seeker. Her actions were sure. Chloe pushed open the door to the parking lot. It had almost seemed like she was on a mission.

But maybe that's what the serial killer believed—that she was on a mission of some kind.

Jake pulled up and rolled down the window. "I hear I'm supposed to be watching out for you today."

She sighed and smiled. Seeing him made her smile and how was that for a kick in the gut? Someone should just shoot her because she wasn't falling for a preacher, not even one as cute as Jake. "Actually, no. I'm supposed to be watching out for you."

"We'll just have to see about that."

She looked around the parking lot. The hair on the back of her neck stood on end. She and Jake could watch out for each other, but someone else was watching them. Someone who wanted to do them harm.

She could feel it.

Jake turned the radio up and rolled the windows down so he could feel the ocean breeze. He wouldn't have to try and avoid her today, at least. If Chloe'd been tasked with protecting him, she'd only follow him. He knew she was more than competent, she was born to be a cop.

That didn't mean he couldn't be extra vigilant, putting himself between her and any danger he might bring her way. He couldn't avoid her. But he could do everything in his power to keep her safe.

A balmy, almost springlike breeze wafted in. "I love it when we get a really warm day this time of year. It reminds me summer's on the way."

Chloe turned her face toward the window and sighed. "Where are we headed?"

"Look in the back." He'd filled a big wicker basket full of gallon-sized plastic bags of cookies.

She laughed. "What are all those?"

He glanced back to the left and turned his blinker on. "Well, my grandma taught me to bake cookies for stress relief, but some weeks I end up with dozens of cookies. So, I started taking them to the shut-ins. Like—"

"Your grandma did." She finished his sentence for him. "Nice."

"Yeah?" He kept his eyes on the road, but his cheek jumped as he tensed his jaw. Maybe she thought his making cookies was girly or silly, but because physical activities had always calmed him, he didn't use a mixer. And that made baking cookies manly.

It wasn't quite as good as pumping iron with the guys from his crew, which he also did twice a week, but it gave him a good excuse to go visiting. He prayed he wasn't bringing danger with him to these precious older members of his congregation. He couldn't lock himself in his office, though sometimes that seemed like the most logical thing to do. More than anything he wanted to check on them—to see for himself that the arsonist hadn't made a move on the most vulnerable in his care.

"It's cool that your grandma taught you stuff." Chloe snagged a bag from the back and pulled out a snickerdoodle, stuffing it in her mouth.

"I think so." He glanced at her and grinned as he pulled into the driveway next to her house—well, Bayley's house. "Mrs. Phillips is up first. She's been a force to be reckoned with in the community for years, but she took a tumble down the stairs this winter and hasn't been able to get out much lately."

She chewed and swallowed. "Whoa. I need milk. Mrs. P., right?"

He threw another look at her, this one surprised. "Profiling again?"

"I wish I was that good. Bayley gave me the rundown on the neighborhood. She said I never had to worry about anyone trying to break into the house. Mrs. P. is like a one-woman neighborhood watch."

He chuckled as he grabbed a couple different bags of cookies from the back. "That's about it."

A long while after the knock, the door swung open to reveal a diminutive lady with a fuzz of black curly hair and a wide, welcoming smile. "Well, Jake Rollins, about time you showed up for coffee. I haven't seen you in at least a week. I was beginning to think you'd forgotten about this old lady."

"You know better than that, Mrs. P.—we swap e-mail jokes every day. This is…"

"Ah, my new neighbor. Chloe, right? I've seen you

around for a few days. How are you, sweetie? You want some coffee or tea?"

Chloe blinked, processed, and said, "Coffee would be great. Let me guess, you've been talking to Bayley Conyers?"

"She keeps me up-to-date on what's going on around town since I can't get out and about like I used to." She looked at them speculatively. "She didn't tell me you two had a little thing for each other, though."

Jake needed to nip that hypothesis in the bud before Mrs. P. had them engaged and a date set and the whole membership of her garden club planning the wedding. He didn't know where things were going, but he sure didn't want Sea Breeze's most intuitive matchmaker sending Chloe away in a panic before she could figure things out on her own.

"Chloe's here on a case, Mrs. P. She's with the FBI. Would you like some cookies with your coffee?" He took her arm and gently eased her toward her favorite recliner, her multicolored strands of glass beads clinking as she walked.

"Of course. Did you bring me some of those with chocolate chips and pecans?"

"Yep. And snickerdoodles, too."

She sighed as he placed a plate on the table beside her. "You are a good boy, Jake. I've missed being at church."

"We've missed you, too." He poured a mug of coffee and settled closest to Mrs. P., noting that Chloe, maybe a little out of her comfort zone, perched on the arm at the other end of the sofa.

Mrs. P. sent a shrewd look at Chloe with her slightly rheumy eyes. "If it would make you feel better, you can pretend I'm a witness and you're interrogating me."

A genuine smile spread across Chloe's face. "That obvious, huh? I'm not exactly used to social visits. I could pretend you're a mob boss and I'm trying to infiltrate your organization."

"I love it." Mrs. P. chortled as she pulled her coffee closer on the side table. "Don't you worry, sweetie. I had to break Jake in, too. He was green when he first came to the ministry from the fire department. But after some rigorous training, he's about got it figured out now."

The old lady giggled and patted his hand. It was no wonder he loved her. She did remind him of his grandmother. Feisty and opinionated and so rich in her faith that it was a pleasure to be around her.

"We've gotten those boys you told me about into the after-school program at Community Fellowship. You were right, Mrs. P., the chance to mentor younger kids turned them right around."

"I figured it would work. They're not bad boys, they just needed some direction. Now instead of vandalizing property, they can teach little kids about basketball."

Chloe smiled at Mrs. P. "Were you by chance in law enforcement?"

"Oh, my. No, honey. I was the secretary for thirty years at my home church in Indiana. When my husband died, I moved down south to our beach house and never regretted it for a minute. But let me tell you, you learn how to pay attention to people when you're the church secretary."

Jake yelped. "What is that?"

He reached under the couch and pulled out a tiny needle-clawed kitten. Gray and white, with a fluffy plume of a tail, the minuscule creature hissed at him. "What kind of ferocious beast have you sicced on me, Mrs. P.?"

Mrs. P. reached over with gentle hands to rescue her baby, who began a ragged purring almost immediately. "Bayley brought her over the other day. Someone had abandoned a whole litter at the drugstore. Can you imagine? This wee one just needs some love."

Jake reached for one gnarled and age-spotted hand and held it lightly between his much bigger ones. "You're just the person to give it to her. Is there anything I can do for you while I'm here?"

"No, honey. All I need is to know that someone cares that this old lady is still in the world and having a cup of coffee and a cookie with you is a sweet reminder that you do care."

"The church cares about you, too, so if you need anything, you call. Okay?"

Mrs. Phillips cuddled the kitten to her chest. "I promise. Chloe, I'll be keeping an eye on things for you. Don't you worry about that."

"Thanks, I appreciate it." The phone at her hip beeped. She silenced it. "I need to get this. Mrs. P., it was lovely meeting you."

He watched as she walked out the door in her tidy business suit and heels. She wasn't anything like he'd expected to find. And yet…and yet.

"Amazing isn't it, how love broadsides you when

you least expect it?" Mrs. P.'s soft voice interrupted his thoughts.

He nearly choked on his coffee. "What makes you think I'm in love with her?"

She laughed. "Oh, Jake. You wanted me to meet her, didn't you?"

He sighed, realizing the best way to stop gossip here was with honesty. "Let's put it this way. I *could* fall for her. But I want a home and a family—that's no secret, especially to you. I'm not sure she wants that."

"Maybe you'd be surprised at what she wants." The old lady rubbed the tiny kitten, smoothing the silky fur into place. "She might even be surprised herself."

Jake crouched in front of Mrs. P. and laid one hand on her shoulder. After praying for her recovery, he stood to leave. "I'll see you soon. You take care of yourself?"

"Of course I will. You, too, my boy. I'll be praying for you."

He ignored the lump in his throat and kissed her fuzzy head. "I love you. You're my favorite, you know."

She giggled. "I bet you say that to all the old ladies. But I love you, too, you scoundrel. Now get out there and take care of things. Next time I see you I want some pecan sandies."

He laughed. "Yes, ma'am."

Pushing the door open, he found Chloe on the porch, a serious expression on her face. "Maria thinks she may have found something on the video. We need to head to the lab."

* * *

Chloe waited impatiently for the elevator to the basement lab. The state-of-the-art facility was shared by the SBPD and the Emerald County sheriff's department. Sharing the facility wasn't usually a problem. Sharing the expertise of Maria Fuentes usually turned out to be more of an issue, or so she'd heard.

Jake had stopped at the reception desk to chat with the officer of the day. Chloe pressed the down button again and glanced down the long gray hall. Cops were so inspired in their decor.

Gabe Sloan stepped into place beside her. "You know, pressing the button multiple times doesn't really speed the elevator up."

She sent him the look that had put more than one criminal on the ground.

Gabe just smiled blandly as the elevator arrived, waving her on board ahead of him. She pressed the button for the basement, just once, and crossed her arms. She hadn't prayed in a long time, but she really wanted to. A strong desire welled in her to ask God to help them get this case solved. Too many people had been hurt, too many lives upended by a killer intent on playing games. Who knew how many more lives would be at risk in the future if they didn't put this arsonist away?

She didn't know if it would do any good. God hadn't heard her prayers when she was a little girl. But maybe she just thought he hadn't heard them. Maybe it was the people in her life that hadn't listened. And God had been there all along.

It was all so difficult to figure out. She sighed impatiently and stuck her hand under her elbow to keep herself from pushing the button again.

Jake slid through the closing doors at the last second. "I didn't miss anything, did I?"

"Just Chloe trying to jam up the elevator system." Gabe crossed his arms and leaned against the back wall.

Mock horror colored Jake's expression. "A button presser?"

Gabe nodded sadly. "I'm afraid so. Most people outgrow that in middle school, but not our Chloe."

The doors slid open at the basement level. Chloe walked out, talking over her shoulder. "Very funny, guys. You should do stand-up on the weekends. I wouldn't quit your day job, though."

They were teasing, of course, and that didn't faze Chloe. It was the words Gabe had used: *not our Chloe.* Those words implied belonging, friendship, teamwork. Even in the Serial Crimes Unit, she hadn't found that same kind of easy acceptance. She blew out a breath, her emotions mixing up inside her. About God, friends, *Jake.*

The handsome preacher had made more than a dent in the lockup that had been her heart.

Gabe slid his ID card through the lock and the doors to the lab slid open. "Maria Fuentes, front and center."

Maria rolled out from behind a work station, her wild curls tied back with some kind of tubing and protective glasses over her eyes. "Slow down, hopscotch. The Sloan name does not automatically take you to the head of the line. Give me two seconds to finish this and I'm all yours."

Gabe dropped into an empty computer chair. "Fine, I'll catch a nap. I'm saving up for when the baby comes."

Jake wandered toward a row of slides, each one with a different type of jelly bean beside it. He reached out a finger.

"Don't. Touch. Anything." Maria didn't turn around, didn't even glance at him.

Jake jerked his finger back, sending Chloe a chastened schoolboy look.

Gabe didn't open his eyes. "She sees everything."

Maria rolled back toward them, shooing Jake toward the computer station as she got there first, her fingers flying over the keys. "Okay, here's what we were able to retrieve from the footage. She had a hat on, but you knew that already. We've got the logo on the hat here." She pointed to a logo that looked like a heron standing in tall grass.

"In this shot, she's bending her head forward, so when I zoom in and enhance, you can see her hair color is streaked blond and brown. For this next one, you owe me a big box of Godiva. I like the milk chocolate." Fuentes waited until Gabe reluctantly nodded, then flashed a quick grin. "Our suspect has a tattoo at the base of her neck. It's only visible briefly—" she pointed "—here. But I snapped and enhanced it. Voilà."

There on the screen, Chloe could see the image of two swords and a scroll, almost covered by her shirt, except for that brief moment. She glanced at Jake. His eyes were narrowed in concentration. "Do you recognize that tat?"

"It looks familiar, but I can't place it on a person." He shrugged.

"Can you print those, Maria? I want to get copies out to the cops as soon as possible."

Maria whirled around in her rolling chair with a manila envelope in her hand, one for Gabe and one for Chloe. "Already done. And I e-mailed them to you."

Chloe stared at Maria. "You're frighteningly efficient."

"Saves time." She whizzed back to the workstation where something was beeping.

Gabe motioned them to the door. "That's her signal that we're dismissed. She's probably already forgotten we're here."

Jake walked over to the spunky forensic specialist. "Thanks, Maria. Don't stay locked up in here all weekend. Family Ministries is throwing a cookout on the beach tomorrow evening."

"Thanks, but I'm not a family."

"Hey, you're part of mine. And regardless, it's for everyone." He tugged at her makeshift ponytail.

She smiled, pulled her protective glasses off again and looked up. "Okay, okay. I'll try to get the guys here to cover for me for a couple of hours. See ya later, Preacher."

Chloe waited for him at the door. He really had a way with people, which she told him as he passed her and the doors swished shut behind them, sealing Maria in her own little fiefdom again.

"Not really, I just like people." His arm brushed against hers as they got on the elevator and made her want to move closer, be closer.

"Is that what makes you a good pastor?"

He kind of laughed. "I don't know if I am a good one."

"You are." Gabe inserted himself into their conversation from the back of the elevator car.

Jake looked at his feet.

"You're not going to try that 'aw-shucks' thing, are you?" Chloe punched him lightly.

"No. But the way things have been going lately, I think the church might be better off without me as their leader."

The elevator shuddered to a stop and Gabe reached for the button to hold the door open. "Jake, these last few days have been enough to make anyone question his calling, but don't ever doubt that you're doing an amazing job."

Gabe stuck his fist out and Jake knocked it with his own, a face-saving gesture for Jake, and Chloe wondered if Gabe knew Jake was fighting embarrassment over telling them his feelings.

"I'm going upstairs to start working my contacts here. If you get anything, call me." Gabe released the button and the elevator closed.

Chloe pushed out of the police precinct into the sunlight. Turning her face into it seemed the most natural thing in the world. The soft air of this little beach town was so different from the tautness of the D.C., which always seeming to be teeming with activity just under the surface. She loved the city, any city, and she'd lived in a bunch. The constant tension, the sense of people going somewhere—it always energized her.

But there was something here. Despite the uneasy

stress of being on guard against a killer, the slower pace of life here had its appeal. There was a sense of life being bigger than her own world, which she tended to get caught up in.

A sense of being closer to God.

Fingers twined with hers, then just as quickly loosened. Surprised, she looked at Jake, but he was looking the other direction, toward the ocean several blocks away.

He cleared his throat. "I'm terrified to hold your hand, afraid that some crazy woman will see me and make taking you away from me her mission in life."

"I'm not scared."

"I know." He shook his head as he opened the door to his 4Runner for her. "But I'm afraid I wouldn't be able to protect you. And that would kill me."

Chloe gulped in air as Jake rounded the back of the car, slid into the driver's seat and just sat, his hand on the steering wheel.

The heavy, superheated air inside the car made her skin feel sensitive and tender, much like she felt on the inside. Much like Jake must feel after an admission like that.

She reached for the hand lying on his thigh, linking her fingers with his. "Hey. We're going to be okay. You *and* me. We're both going to be fine because we're going to get this woman. We're going to take her down and she's going to spend the rest of her life in jail. And then we'll figure out this, whatever this is."

A smile ghosted across his face. He lifted her hand

to his lips. "*This* is me falling for an amazing, strong, talented woman. You can take that however you want to, but you need to know I fully intend to see it through when this is over."

She blinked, stunned by his admission. In the very same instant, she felt joy and utter terror. He was such a remarkable man, never taking the easy way, always making a stand, always stepping out in faith. Couldn't she at least meet him halfway?

"*Okay.*" She blew a breath out.

In her jacket pocket was the tiny slip of paper from the fortune cookie. *The time is right to make new friends.*

She hadn't believed it, but so wanted it to be true that she'd been carrying it around in her pocket as a memory. What if…he was right about this, too?

It was so far out there she almost couldn't grasp it. She couldn't imagine one place, one *person* always being in her life. Even if it was what she wanted.

"Okay. I can deal with that." She squeezed his fingers as she looked around the parking lot. "But for now I'm getting antsy just sitting in one spot. Can you drop me at the house before you go back to work?"

"You got it." He put the SUV in Reverse.

She shivered, the feeling of someone watching them creeping up the back of her neck. "We're going to catch her, Jake. We're getting close, I can feel it."

ELEVEN

Jake plowed through the e-mail in his in-box, but his mind was with Chloe searching for a killer. Logically, he knew that she didn't need him for this part of the search and that with a uniformed cop posted outside the beach house she was as safe as she could be.

What he'd said in the elevator to Gabe and Chloe—maybe he did need to let the church go on without him, at least for a while. As word leaked the women in town had become afraid to come to services. The one place that should be their refuge had become a place of fear.

He tunneled his fingers through his hair. It wasn't fair, but he could manage. And maybe they'd figure something out soon.

The intercom on his desk beeped. "Hey, Susan."

"Jake, there's a woman here to see you. Elaine Barbury?"

"Are you going to be here a little while longer?"

"Yes, I'll be here at least another half hour, and I'm pretty sure Sean's in the youth ministry office."

"Okay, Suse, send her on back. Thanks." He slid the

mass of stuff to the side, trying to clear at least a small space in the middle of his desk.

A few seconds later, he heard a tentative knock. "Come on in, Elaine."

He crossed the room to greet her at the door, making sure to leave it open a crack. She walked into his office, giving his collection of communion cups a curious once-over before abruptly turning back to him, shoving a box tied with string at his stomach. "I heard you like cookies."

Wow. He walked around his desk to sit down and gestured for her to do the same. "I do. This is very sweet of you, Elaine."

"Well, you're always sayin' thanks to people on Sundays, you know, for bringin' you stuff and I thought maybe that's what people were supposed to do." She didn't really meet his eyes, just looked from one side of his office to the other.

She was acting very strange, but dealing with strange people wasn't really anything new for him. The big question was, what brought her here? What was at the heart of her visit?

"Thank you for thinking of me, but you're welcome here anytime. No gifts necessary." He smiled at her.

"You've been real nice to me, Pasto—uh—Jake." Her gaze caught his and she looked away again.

"What can I do for you, Elaine?"

"I've been coming to church some and I like it. I don't feel like everybody's looking at me here." She stared at the floor and went very quiet for a minute. "I hear you talk about God and all, like He's the Father of us all. Pastor Jake, my dad left us when I was a little girl and it really messed my mom and me up. Having a father just doesn't sound that good to me."

Jake took a deep breath, and silently, almost instinctively, prayed for the right words to say. "A lot of people have been deeply wounded by their earthly father, Elaine. I guess you could say I'm one of them." He let that sink in a little. "There are no easy answers, but having God on your side is like being adopted by the father you wish you'd had."

She tilted her head, thinking. "Maybe I want to know that God."

He slid out one of his desk drawers, pulled a sheet of paper out of a file and handed it to her. "There are lots of names for God in the Bible. *God of salvation, God the provider, God of forgiveness, God of justice.* Those are just a few, but they help me remember that God the Father is so many things to me that my own dad definitely wasn't. He fills the places my dad just wasn't able to fill."

She blinked quickly as she folded the sheet in her hands. "I know you had a hard time when your fiancée died and you didn't get to be a firefighter anymore, but it looks like you've gotten through it okay."

"Everybody has tough times, Elaine. Knowing God doesn't mean that we won't still have them. But it does mean that we won't go through them alone."

Her brownish-blond hair had fallen forward to almost cover her face. "I used to see you fighting fires."

Watching. Jake fought off the creepy feeling. Elaine was struggling, just like anyone else who came through those office doors. "Yeah?"

"I like to watch fires a lot. My dad was an EMT."

Maybe that explained things. And maybe it gave her a reason to start the fires. "Elaine, do you set fires so you can watch them?"

Her head jerked up. "No." She hesitated. "But I don't always do good things, Pastor Jake."

"Do you want to tell me about it?" He wouldn't push—that wasn't his job. It was his job to ask if she needed help, and to suggest places she could get some.

She shook her head, her eyes firmly on the floor.

"I'm not accusing you of anything, Elaine. If you feel closer to your dad by watching the firefighters, I can understand that. Maybe it would help you if you talked about your past to someone understanding."

"Like you?" She whispered it, without looking up.

"I don't counsel much. I'm not really qualified." He reached in the desk drawer and handed her a card. "Here's the name of a woman in town. She's excellent. I think you'll like her."

Elaine crumpled the card and stuffed it and the sheet he'd given her in her jeans pocket as she stood. "I've gotta be going now. I'll think about what you said."

Jake got up to open the door for her, while she leaned over to pick up her purse. Transfixed, he stared at the back of her neck.

She glanced up. "What?"

He swallowed hard, forced a smile. "Nothing, just

lost my train of thought for a second, thinking about those cookies you brought, I guess."

For just a moment, she smiled, and he would've sworn it was genuine and sincere.

"I think you're nice, um, Jake. And I hope you like the cookies."

"Bye, Elaine."

He watched out the window until she got into the parking lot and then picked up the phone to call Chloe. It rang in his hand. Startled, he almost dropped it.

"Hello?"

Chloe's voice held a hint of controlled excitement. "I found her."

He sat down hard in his desk chair. "Elaine Barbury."

"How did you know?"

"She was just here. I saw the tattoo on the back of her neck, exactly like the photo." Adrenaline kicked in his system at the thought of it, that she'd been sitting in his office.

"Jake! Are you okay?"

"I'm fine. But I've got a box of cookies we should probably have processed for the same opiates that were in the other ones."

"Don't touch them. I'll be there in just a minute. I need to let Gabe know that Elaine just left there. He'll get the uniforms on it."

Jake heard her phone slap shut. He stabbed both hands into his hair, just letting his head drop. He hadn't breached a confidence, so why did he feel so guilty? Maybe because Elaine seemed to be truly seeking answers. And being so socially awkward, it had been extremely difficult for her to come here in the first place.

She'd made the decision to set the explosives on the range and put a bomb under Chloe's car. It wasn't up to him now.

Chloe barreled into Jake's office. "Jake! The door was unlocked again."

She saw him sitting at his desk, his head in his hands, and stopped. "Jake?"

He lifted his head and the raw emotion she saw in his eyes gripped her in its intensity. She sat slowly on the edge of his office chair. "Hey."

"Hey."

His voice sounded so unbelievably tired. She had a weird urge to take him in her arms and hold him, and since touchy-feely wasn't her thing, the impulse surprised her. But this wasn't like Jake. He'd been through so much and had held strong. "What did Elaine Barbury want with you?"

If possible, the lines of grief on his face went even deeper. He shook his head. "The information isn't pertinent to the case."

"Anything about the fires?"

"No. Other than she admitted to being there before, when I was a firefighter. Her dad was an EMT. She watches at the scenes because it's a memory."

"Okay." She stretched the word out, thinking. "We know she planted the explosives at the range. According to her background, she had the knowledge to set the bomb under my car, but did she know it was my car? Was she targeting me?"

"I don't know."

"Come on, Jake. You know people. Did you get the sense that she could murder Julie and Sharon?"

He blew out a breath, scrubbing a hand over his face. "I wish I could tell you. She's ill at ease in normal conversation and obviously she has issues. But murder? I don't know if I could say that."

"It's very possible that she's lost touch with reality. I could see that she was a little edgy the other day. Add an abusive background?" She let her voice drift up in question.

He tilted his head. "Maybe abused. At the very least her father was absent."

Chloe nodded slowly. "It fits."

"She brought me cookies, Chloe. She thinks I'm nice." He paused, sadness evident on his face. "As creepy as she acts, I feel like I'm betraying her."

Chloe leaned forward so he would hear what she was saying. "Either way, she needs help, Jake. I'll do my best to see that she gets it."

He looked into her eyes and nodded slowly. "You're gonna want these." He pushed a string-tied box toward her.

She looked warily at the box. "Maybe we better have the bomb squad look at it."

He groaned. "I'm seriously going to have to give up cookies."

She stood, laughing, and grabbed his hand, reaching for the cell phone at her waist with the other one.

"Unless you make them yourself. Those are the best ones, anyway. Come on, we'll leave that thing for the big boys. They should be here any minute. Let's head to the station and see what Gabe's got for us."

The uniforms had brought Elaine in.

Jake stood at the window of the interview room and watched her as she sat chained to the table. Out in the hall, Chloe talked with Gabe about how they would proceed with her.

Elaine couldn't see Jake, but she had a wild look in her eye as she stared into the mirrored glass on her side of the window. She would alternately screw her eyes into tiny slits and shake her head, as if trying to wake herself up.

Something bad had happened to Elaine to mess her up this way. And as angry as he was about what had happened to Julie and to Sharon, even Anna, he couldn't help but have compassion for Elaine. Something damaged her, something so terrible that she couldn't deal with it, except to act out in harmful ways. *Oh, God, please help her find peace.*

Chloe pushed into the room where Jake stood watching Elaine, a thin file folder in her hand. She'd added a jacket to her dress pants and tiny white T-shirt and looked every bit the FBI agent. She had her hair tied back in a smooth ponytail and a pencil tucked behind her ear. She stopped briefly at the door to the interview room, took a deep breath, gave Jake a quick thumbs-up and entered the room.

Chloe sat opposite Elaine, her voice coming clearly through the speaker in the observation room. "Ms. Barbury, we've met before. I'm Supervisory Special Agent Chloe Davis, with the FBI. We kept you waiting—I'm so sorry we were rude."

From an elastic ring on her wrist, she pulled a tiny key and released Elaine from the cuffs. Within seconds, Elaine's shoulders dropped and she relaxed just slightly in the chair.

Gabe slid back into the room. "What'd I miss?"

"Nothing yet. What's going on?"

White teeth flashed in the semidark room. "In the middle of chasing down our best suspect, I got a call from Sailor. She was at the hospital."

Jake gaped. "Dude, what are you doing here?"

"It's a normal pregnancy thing. No big deal. The doctor told her to stay off her feet for the rest of the day." He crossed his arms and made a face. "But she wants doughnuts for dinner. I'll never understand pregnant women."

Chloe continued her silence for another moment, studying Elaine as the other woman wilted under the scrutiny. When Chloe spoke, she softened her voice. "Elaine, I don't think you're a bad person."

Elaine shook her head without looking up.

"I think some bad things have happened to you in your life. Tell me about the army captain who took advantage of your friend."

Elaine lifted her head. Her face was slack with shock. "Nobody was supposed to be able to find out about that."

"You weren't supposed to tell, were you?" Chloe pulled a piece of paper out of the file and slid it in front of Elaine.

Gabe elbowed Jake. "Where does she get this stuff?"

"She did research. Called in some favors at the Pentagon, I think." He stared through the window at Elaine, willing her to talk.

"I had to sign some papers, like that one." Elaine shrugged, her mouth twisting with contempt. "Captain Rogers made Rebecca's life a living nightmare. He tortured her from the time she got to work until the time she went to bed. And sometimes, he would call her all night long, just to tell her how he was going to make her miserable the next day."

"What happened to Rebecca, Elaine?"

In the observation room, Jake shifted restlessly. "What does this have to do with the murders?"

Gabe shushed him. "She's building trust and laying the groundwork for Elaine's future actions."

Chloe spoke again, her quiet, sure voice enticing Elaine to tell her story. Jake held his breath.

Elaine looked at her hands, twisting them together on the steel table. "She killed herself."

Jake started. "What did she say?"

"Her friend killed herself. That was probably what pushed her over the edge." Gabe shrugged out of his jacket, tossed it on a chair.

Chloe leaned forward. "And that made you sad, and angry. I understand. I would've wanted to kill Captain Rogers."

Elaine scratched her head, looked away. "I didn't kill him."

Chloe sat back, tilted her head, studied Elaine's face. "I know. You blew up his garage."

Elaine shot to her feet. "He deserved it. He deserved to die."

Heart in his throat, Jake reached for the doorknob. Gabe grabbed his arm. "Hold on. Let her handle it."

Chloe tapped the papers in her file into a neat stack. "Elaine, please sit down."

Slowly, Elaine eased into a rigid seated position.

"What did you think when Randy Keane asked you out? Were you mistrustful because he was former military?"

"I thought he was a nice guy. Not like that weasel Rogers."

"So when Randy Keane didn't want to date you anymore, didn't even want you coming to the range…you decided that he deserved what he got, too?"

"I wanted to bring my Stechkin APS. It's a collector's item." Elaine rolled her eyes. "Well, it's a *shooting* range, isn't it?"

Chloe slid another picture across the table. She was so cool under pressure. Jake was sweating bullets watching her, but she made her job look easy.

"What is this?" Their suspect barely glanced at the photo.

"That's my car, Elaine. And the figure underneath it? That's you, planting C-4. You know a little about plastic explosives from your army days, don't you?"

The whites of her eyes showing, Elaine, with shaking fingers, shoved her blunt-cut hair behind her ears. "I know about explosives. I didn't know that was your car."

Her voice deceptively soft, Chloe said, "Elaine, I don't think you wanted to kill Randy. I think you wanted to make some noise, scare him a little like you did Captain Rogers."

"I swear I didn't know that was your car." Elaine had crossed her arms over her ribs and trembled.

"Okay, I believe you. So I want you to answer this honestly. Why did you try to kill Anna Prentiss?"

Without saying another word, Chloe leaned over and pulled an evidence bag out of her purse. She slid it across the table. Jake caught the gleam of the *E* charm. *E for Elaine.*

Elaine's trembling lips firmed into a hard line. "I can kill whoever I want whenever I want. You police think you're so smart. You have no idea what I'm capable of."

Chloe shrugged. "Explain it to me, Elaine. You told me the other day that if you wanted to take revenge on someone that he would never see it coming."

"Well, it looks like someone's gotten the last laugh on me, doesn't it?"

"What does that mean, Elaine?" When she didn't answer, Chloe went on. "We have evidence and we have priors that suggest predisposition to this type of crime. Elaine, did you kill Julie Mansford and Sharon Hardin and set the fire that nearly killed Anna Prentiss?"

Again Elaine didn't answer. She stared into the window. Jake knew she couldn't see him, but it seemed as if she were staring right into his eyes. The pain and hurt that he saw in hers nearly knocked him over.

"Elaine?"

"You've got it all figured out. You tell me." She stared at the window, right at Jake. She was hurting so badly. He began to pray for her, instinctively knowing that the pain and damage were so deep only God could reach her there.

Chloe didn't move. She didn't take her eyes of Elaine. "I think you killed Julie Mansford. You killed Sharon Hardin. I think you attempted to kill Anna Prentiss and you set explosives at Randy Keane's property. I also think you're going to jail for a long, long time."

Elaine picked up the evidence bag that held the charm. "*E* for Elaine, hmm? You didn't find a chain?"

"No."

She tossed the bag back to the table. "Fine, take me away. I confess."

Chloe narrowed her eyes. "To what?"

"To everything. Anything you say. I did it. I did it all and some things you didn't even mention."

Chloe pulled a blank sheet of paper from the pile and pushed it across the table. "Write down what you did. Write down why you did it. Every detail you can remember. And sign it."

Chloe pushed away from the table. With her hand on the doorknob, she looked back. Elaine hadn't moved. The paper sat blank on the table. Jake knew he should feel relieved that they had caught the person that had been tormenting not only him but their whole town. Instead he felt sad.

* * *

Chloe opened the door to the observation room. Now that she wasn't facing Elaine Barbury, she felt the exhaustion in every inch of her body. All she wanted to do was go home and sleep off the weariness. Unfortunately, she couldn't do that.

Gabe held out a fist for Chloe to punch. "Awesome job, Chloe. A killer off the streets and a victory for our joint task force."

She lifted a hand. "I think celebrations would be a little premature. Let's wait and see if she actually knows what she's confessing to. She didn't actually admit to anything."

Gabe stepped back, blinked. "Yes, she did. I heard her say, 'I confess to everything.'"

"Given what she's been through, I wouldn't doubt that she has a persecution complex. She'll admit to anything just to get us to leave her alone."

Gabe threw his hands in the air. "Of course she did the crimes. She confessed. We have her on tape. We have the charm with an *E* on it. I repeat, *she confessed*. You've done great with this whole case, Chloe. And I have to hand it to you, you called it when you said our perp was a female. But I'm pretty sure you're over-thinking this."

She looked from one to the other, seeing the hope there that this nightmare would be over. She wanted it to be over. For Jake's sake.

Chloe tapped her foot. "Do you have the warrant for her residence?"

Gabe grinned. "Got the crime-scene unit there as we speak."

"I want to see it. And if we find motive, you can call it closed."

"Done." Gabe opened the door for her.

She hesitated, catching Jake's eyes.

"We've got that community-wide church picnic later today, so I really need to get over to the church. I'll see you in a couple of hours." The corner of his mouth tugged up in an increasingly endearing smile, the dimple deepening into a dent, his eyes telling her so much more than his words. Whatever was between them still needed to be said.

"See you later." Chloe followed Gabe out the door to check out Elaine's house, hoping for answers, but definitely willing to settle for evidence.

Two hours later, the team had searched every cranny of Elaine's house and hadn't found one shred of evidence. Chloe walked the outside perimeter. Elaine had been in Iraq. She'd spent time in Afghanistan. It was possible that she'd learned some tricks about hiding while she was there.

No telltale air vents around the base of the foundation indicated a hidden basement. She rounded the corner of the house and walked the length of the garage to the front where it stood open. Nothing.

There were no locked cabinets, no strange places in the wall. She walked into the garage where Gabe stood chatting with Maria Fuentes. "Nothing?"

"Nada." Maria sipped from a can of Diet Coke. "The problem is we know she had the shotgun and the rounds she used to set the range on fire and it's not here."

Chloe looked around. "Maybe she rented a storage unit somewhere away from her home."

Gabe scowled. "I've got people going through her receipts, but it'll take a while."

"Wait." Chloe walked toward the back of the garage where a workbench lined the wall. "Wait, wait, wait."

She'd walked the length outside, but the distance inside seemed much shorter. So if the inside length were shorter, that meant… She crouched to look under the workbench and tugged at a leather strap. A small door swung open.

Gabe shouted behind her as she scooched through the small opening. Carefully, wary of any booby trap that might be there, she peered into the tiny room, shining her flashlight around the walls. What she saw made her freeze. A collection of firearms lined one wall. Not only the shotgun Elaine had used to ignite the fuel canisters and the fully automatic pistol that she hadn't been allowed to shoot at the range, but at least a dozen more highly collectible weapons. On the opposite wall hung a poster-sized picture of Jake in firefighter gear. Tacked around it were smaller photos of him and the other firefighters.

Not exactly proof, but with her confession and the other circumstantial evidence, it was enough to put Elaine away.

Chloe ducked out and held the flashlight up to Gabe. "Take a look."

A few seconds inside were all he needed. She could tell by the expression on his face that he'd come to the same conclusion even before he said the words. "It's over now."

She nodded slowly.

"Sometimes people aren't as complicated as we try to make them, Chloe. And the person who confesses is usually the one who actually committed the crimes." He had a fierce glint to his eye. "This case is closed."

Chloe slid onto the round bar stool in Sailor's coffee shop, the familiar earthy scent of the coffee soothing her ragged temper.

Pregnant Sailor took one look at her face, added another shot to the latte she was building and skimmed it across the glossy black countertop to Chloe.

"Thanks." Chloe cradled the warm mug in her hands, blowing across the slightly foamy surface of the latte.

"No problem. Rough day?"

She considered. "You could say that."

Sailor waved one of her assistants over and eased her just-starting-to-show-self onto the stool next to Chloe.

"I thought you were supposed to be home with your feet up." Chloe waved a wary hand in the region of Sailor's belly.

"Pshh—that was Gabe's nonsense. The doctor said I'm fine." She pulled her mug of tea closer, sent Chloe a speculative look. "So, other than the case trying to swallow you whole, what's bothering you?"

"We closed the case." Chloe stared into her coffee, as

if she'd find the secret there to why she still felt so crummy. Maybe it had something to do with the phone call she'd gotten from her boss about their new assignment.

Sailor grinned. "So, this funk has something to do with a certain tall handsome pastor, one who happens to look hot in turnout gear?"

Chloe didn't smile, couldn't. "Am I so obvious, then?"

"Let's just put it this way. That sick, uncertain look on your face could have been transplanted from mine a few months ago." Sailor rubbed at a spot on the granite with the sleeve of her shirt.

Chloe didn't move. "He's had such a tough time with this case. I wish things were different, that I could make it all go away for him."

"Don't you think having you here to go through it with him has helped?"

"I don't know, Sailor. I'm not exactly the friend type. And I guess that's what's got me bummed more than anything. My job is really important to me…but I do like Jake."

"Good girl. Admitting you have a problem is the first step." Sailor held her mug out for Chloe to clink.

Chloe couldn't resist a little chuckle. "Oh, yeah, cheers. You know, I've never been the sticking type, Sailor. I don't have family or even normal friendships. I've had handlers. Suspects that I had to get close to and build relationships with." She smothered a twinge of guilt at the thought that once upon a time Sailor had been one of those. "But I don't have friends. Never been anyplace long enough to have them."

Sailor's smile grew wider. "I beg to differ. Honey, I hate to tell you, but you and I are friends."

Chloe's eyes snapped back to meet Sailor's earnest green ones, before skimming back to the walls and Sailor's funky art collection.

Sailor nodded, her lips pursed in thought. "What would happen if I called you in Virginia and told you that I needed help? Wouldn't you come?"

"Yes, but…"

"But, nothing. You're a friend. And you've got friends here in Sea Breeze, Chloe Davis. Get used to it." Sailor grabbed hold of Chloe's hand with her own, warm from the mug of tea.

Chloe didn't know whether to laugh or cry. Maybe more than anything she felt grief that she had her first girlfriend in her life and she lived nearly a thousand miles away in Quantico, Virginia.

Finally, she squeezed Sailor's hand. "I don't have to come in the birthing room, do I?"

Sailor laughed, her silky stream of blond hair sliding forward to nearly cover her face before she slung it back over her shoulder. "No, hon, Gabe's got that covered." She leaned closer, conspiratorially. "Now. About Jake."

Chloe met her eyes. "I do like Jake. He's an amazingly genuine person. I don't think he knows how rare that is. But I live in Virginia and Jake—needs a cookie-baking wife, not someone like me."

Sailor narrowed her eyes. "Has *Jake* said that?"

An ache began to build in Chloe's chest. "He wants a home and family."

"There are lots of ways to build a family. Gabe and I are living proof of that."

The tightness in Chloe's chest expanded, nearly choking her. "I know you're trying to help, but maybe I'm just not supposed to have a—"

"What? Someone who cares about you? Here's the truth and you need to write it on your heart because it's one you're not going to want to forget. The power of love is an amazing thing."

Chloe forced a smile. "You sound like a talk-show host."

"Maybe so, but believe me, Chloe. You're worth being loved. Jake knows how to bake cookies. Maybe he needs a smart, intuitive wife who can read people. Oh, and shoot a gun. Never know when that'll come in handy." She held her still-smallish belly as she slid off the stool. "Now I need to get my lazy self back to the house. You're going to the picnic at the church in a little while, right?"

A crowd of people looking at her, *really* her, not a made-up person that she was pretending to be? Sounded like her worst nightmare. "Ahh…sure?"

"Good girl."

"Gabe's not going to let you go." Chloe eased off the chair and picked up her bag, making sure her jacket covered her weapon.

"Sure he will. I've already got my lawn chair packed in the car. I'll keep my feet up." Sailor's face radiated the peace and love that she'd found in her relationship with Gabe and her deep faith.

Way down inside, in that place that Chloe didn't even want to admit existed, she longed to know that same peace. It was like she knew what it was, even where to find it, but peace just always seemed a little out of her grasp.

Jake strolled onto the grassy front lawn of the church. Actually, *strolled* would be a bit of an exaggeration. *Limped* would be more accurate, considering he had to work to lift his left leg off the ground. The back injury that had taken him off the fire department had also left him with a pretty good indicator of coming weather. And, while the sky was blue at the moment, the north wind that had kept the temperatures cool this week would probably shift later, causing thunderstorms as the warm gulf air comingled with it.

The worship band played from a makeshift stage and church members had spread blankets in a colorful array. The teenagers were well into their beach volleyball tournament.

The party had been planned to give the church a welcome break from the repairs and to let the town know that they weren't going anywhere despite the blow that had been dealt. It had turned out to be a huge community party, celebrating the capture of the serial arsonist and murderer that had tapped into some of their deepest fears. The fear that their home would be threatened. That somehow they would be next.

A car door slammed behind him. He turned around to see Chloe, gleaming red hair streaming just past her shoulders. She didn't look much like the pin-straight professional this afternoon, in her shorts and baby T. How could someone so tiny have legs that long?

Jake swallowed hard and looked away toward the beach. "It's a little breezy out here. You got a jacket?"

She shrugged into a ragged zip-front hoodie. "I'm not sure what I'm doing here, Jake. This isn't really my thing."

He stepped close to her. "Why did you come?"

"I promised Sailor I would."

Closer, he could smell the sweet vanilla scent underlaid with something spicy that was just…her. It made him want to touch. A wisp of hair trailed across her cheek. He reached for it, letting his fingers skim behind. Her breath quickened just before she took a step away.

"Looks like you have a good turnout."

He smiled. "Practically the whole town came. Even Anna and little Mason are over there."

She followed his line of vision and her lips curved as she recognized Anna with the other moms keeping a close eye as Mason jumped with the little kids in one of those big bouncy houses.

"I should warn you that people have been asking where you are. They all want to talk to the person who took down the woman who has held the town hostage." Jake loved the interaction with the people in his church. It energized him, but he wasn't sure Chloe would enjoy it as much as he did, especially if people were grilling her about the case.

She slowed nearly to a stop, her eyes darting back to his. "That wasn't just me, Jake."

He laced his fingers with hers. "Come on. Just be yourself and it'll be fine."

She walked along beside him, but still wasn't quite the confident, full-of-life Chloe that he'd gotten to know.

He pulled her to a stop by the children's playground. Little kids of all ages climbed all over the multicolored plastic structure. "What's wrong? And don't tell me it's the crowd here because I know it's not just that."

She blew a breath out. "I shouldn't say this, especially to you. I'm just not sure Elaine is the one we've been looking for."

Jake looked around and lowered his voice. "I'm confused. She confessed, right?"

"Yes. And there was more evidence at her house that she had the knowledge needed to commit the crimes." Chloe picked at the sleeve of her hoodie.

"So then…"

"So, I think she's lying. I don't know why. For the attention, or because everyone has always believed the worst of her. Maybe because she wishes she had the guts. I don't know." She looked miserable. "I could also be totally wrong."

"Elaine had motive for the attack at the range, right?" Jake leaned an elbow on the fence, taking the weight off his left leg.

"Yes, and one of sorts for the other crimes, if you take into account that she had a history of revenge seeking and a not-so-secret crush on you. I talked to my boss. He says I'm making this too complicated—that most of the time it's the simple answer and I haven't been doing this long enough to know when to pack it in."

One of the little kids ran up with a flower for Jake. He took the dandelion through the fence and tickled her nose with it. She ran giggling back to the swings. "And Gabe?"

"Gabe closed the case. There was no reason not to." She made a restless movement with her hands. "We have someone who fits the profile in custody and she confessed. Sort of. We'll know more when we get her written statement."

"You'd do the same?"

She bit her lip. "I can't say what I would do. I'm not in Gabe's position."

A huddle of women who'd been chatting by the food table spotted the two of them and surrounded them. One older lady with a jaunty pink polka-dotted scarf tied around her neck slid her arm through Chloe's. "Chloe, right? You must've been working like crazy to find that woman and put her away. We're so lucky that you came to town to help the police department with this case."

"Actually, your police department did the hard work, Mrs...."

"Bennett," Jake supplied helpfully.

The other woman, a slightly younger version, took Chloe's hand on the other side, nudging Jake out of the way. "I'm Sheila Taylor. And I make the best coconut cake in the county."

Chloe barely had time for a backward glance as the two pulled her into the crowd. For the rest of the afternoon he kept a close eye as she was handed off from one group to another, wishing he could shake the uneasy feeling he'd gotten after talking to Chloe. But the truth was, he thought she could be right.

He knew Elaine had problems stemming from her childhood. Other people might get mad and send a nasty e-mail and regret it. Elaine used explosives to exact her revenge. Definitely not normal behavior. Maybe it was her.

From his position grilling chicken, Jake watched as the middle school girls recruited Chloe for their volleyball team. Later he saw her refereeing the soccer game on the sand, nearly having to break up a fight between two kids from opposing high schools. In the end, though they towered over her by at least a foot, she managed to make them shake hands.

He had to say, he was proud of his friends for making her welcome. Yeah, a lot of it was good old-fashioned curiosity, but they were genuinely friendly, too, for the most part.

Finally as the darkness grew, blankets were pulled in close on the grassy lawn where the outside movie screen had been set up. Spotting Chloe trying to slip away, he cut across the yard to meet her. "Got you a spot right over there on my blanket along with a piece of Mrs. Taylor's famous coconut cake."

She sighed, but allowed herself to be led to a quilt he'd spread close to the back of the crowd, a little off to the side from the young families. "It's not that I have anything against *The Princess Bride,* but I'm exhausted."

"All that soccer?"

She looked bemused. "Saw that, huh?"

"You looked pretty competent."

"All-state my senior year in high school." She shrugged, looked away. "I'd have done just about anything to avoid my great-aunt's place. She made it very clear that she was only doing her duty. Soccer practiced five days a week."

"I'm really sorry, Chloe." He stopped at the blanket, gestured for her to sit down.

She dropped to a sitting position. "It's no big deal. Soccer got me to college. I liked being on a team. Liked being athletic."

Jake moved slower, stretching his leg out before easing down to the ground. He gritted his teeth as the muscles in his back snagged up. Payback for all the painting and hauling this week.

"Your back giving you trouble?" Of course she noticed. She rarely missed anything.

"A little. It's really nothing."

She pursed her lips. "Mmm-hmm."

He shoved a plate into her hands. "Here, have some cake. Mrs. Taylor made me promise you would try it."

"Nice deflection." But she took a bite, closing her eyes as creamy goodness exploded in her mouth. He knew from experience.

Jake stared as the expression on her face went from speculative to bliss in a single unguarded second. When her lashes rose, she swallowed hard as she found him still looking at her. "You really are so pretty, Chloe. And you don't have any idea, do you?"

Panic darted into her eyes and the moment was gone. "Stop, Jake, seriously. Don't do this."

He tilted his head, studying her.

But instead of looking at him, she whipped around, looking hard into the stand of trees lining the parking lot. "Did you hear that?"

"No, I…" He stopped, hearing a baby crying.

Before he could finish his sentence, she was on her feet and running toward the woods.

Cursing his bad back, Jake pushed through the haze of pain that narrowed his vision as he jumped up to follow after her. No path existed and what little light remained vanished as he stepped into the trees.

When his eyes adjusted he found Chloe about twenty yards in. She motioned for him to stay still as he got closer, holding up two fingers. How could she see?

The baby's cry only sounded louder, more desperate.

TWELVE

Chloe took in the scene in the clearing. A lean, scruffy-looking man held Mason under one arm. He held Anna at arm's length on the other side.

She leaned close to Jake, breathing words in his ear. "Do you know that guy?"

Jake squinted into the clearing. "I don't, but I'm guessing Anna's ex-boyfriend?"

She watched for a minute. The guy held Mason away from Anna, spinning as she tried to get to him. When she would almost get to the baby, the dude jerked him away from her.

Jake started forward, his muscles bowing under her hand.

"Hey, wait." She grabbed for his arm. "Let's think just for a second. Text Gabe to get in here. I think we need him."

The baby's pitch grew higher. Anna screamed.

"Scratch that." Chloe looked into Jake's eyes. "We don't have time to wait."

Crashing forward through the underbrush, she barreled into the clearing, faking surprise as she startled the man gripping Anna's arm in a punishing hold.

She called back to Jake. "Whoa, babe. Looks like our little love nest is already in use."

Jake walked into the clearing and slid his arm around her waist, his hand curving around her ribs. Her heart, already racing, picked up speed. "Anna, you doing okay?"

The guy, she could see now, was somewhere around twenty years old, with a scraggly goatee and about three days' worth of grime. He answered for Anna. "She's fine. We were just leaving."

"No. We weren't." Anna slung her arms down, breaking the guy's hold, but he still had baby Mason.

Chloe tracked the grimy guy with her eyes as the wind picked up and leaves swirled around them.

Jake angled forward. "What's your name, man?"

The young guy—kid, really—sent Jake a suspicious look and turned so that Mason was nearly hidden behind his back. But he answered. "Ray."

"How long have you and Anna been friends?"

The kid glared at Anna. "Coupla years. Since high school."

Anna sniffed wetly, tears running down her face, her eyes glued on her little son, who still whimpered behind Ray's back. "He's not my friend."

Ray, moving before Chloe could intervene, struck Anna across the cheekbone. Her head snapped to the side and she fell to the ground sobbing. Mason screeched and flailed under Ray's arm.

Chloe forced herself to focus on the attacker, not on

Anna. She couldn't afford to divide her attention, not now. Consciously relaxing her muscles, she made herself look as unimposing as possible. "Ray, why don't we calm down? Let's talk about what you want. We'll try to make it happen for you."

"I am calm." The guy shouted at her, his free arm circling in short, jittery motions. In the darkness, it was hard to see his pupils, but his eyes were red and his nose was running. He was jonesing—she'd bet her last paycheck. "*She* wants to keep my kid away from me."

The odds against them getting out of this without someone getting hurt had just gotten higher, because if he was on something, or coming off something, it would be harder to calm him down. The kid was a powerful motivator for him, whether he genuinely cared about Mason or was just using him to torture Anna. It was possible she'd have to take him down. She'd have to take him by surprise, be quicker and stronger.

But there was the baby to think about.

Jake slid his arm from her back and took a step toward the jittery addict. "I know you're trying to do the right thing. And Anna and Mason, they're your family, right?"

Ray went still, flicked his eyes back to Jake and jerked a nod. "Yeah, so?"

Jake stepped closer. "So, I get it. My dad ditched me when I was a kid. It stinks when the people who are supposed to always be there for you let you down. You don't want to let Mason down. You want to be a dad, right?"

"Yeah." The guy's shoulders dropped a fraction. Mason's cries had quieted to short whimpering breaths.

"This isn't the way to be a good dad, Ray. Think about it. Think about what you're doing."

"I *am* thinking about it. It's her fault." Anna had remained curled in a ball on the ground. Ray moved toward her, telegraphing his intention of hurting her again. Quickly, Chloe drew his attention back.

"Hey. I've got an idea."

He scowled at the sniffling girl on the ground, then dragged his eyes back to Chloe. "Yeah?"

She took one more step toward him, putting him in arm's reach. Being undercover for so many years, she'd learned to place herself in a position of strength without alerting the other person of her intention. She was used to operating with her only weapon being her under-standing of the other person's mind.

She glanced down. "Maybe the kid's crying because he's hungry. There's a table full of food out there. Why don't you let my friend take Mason to get something? Maybe he'll bring you something, too."

Jake cut his eyes at her. No need to wonder what he was thinking. He was thinking she better not be serious about him leaving her here with this guy because there was no way he'd do it. But what he said was, "I bet there's some fried chicken left."

She breathed a small sigh of relief as Ray righted little Mason in his arms. For a long minute Chloe didn't think it would work, but Anna's ex finally loosened his grip. Within seconds, Jake had the little boy in his arms and the hostage element of the dangerous situation had just been defused.

Anna jumped to her feet, going for Jake and the baby. Lightning fast, Ray went to cut her off, his fingers curling into a fist.

Just as fast, Chloe cupped her hands and slapped them against his head. He reeled around, the blow to his ears disorienting to him.

She followed it up with a punch to the chin. He went down and she slammed a knee between his shoulder blades, pinning his arms behind him. "You're under arrest, Ray."

She'd just pulled off her belt and cinched the jerk's hands together when Gabe Sloan crashed into the clearing, slowing when he saw Ray on the ground. He looked up at Chloe and Jake. "Well, it looks like you've got everything under control here."

"You can read him his rights and take him to jail." Chloe grinned.

Gabe jerked Ray to his feet, dragging him into the woods muttering something about Chloe having all the fun.

Chloe lifted Anna back to her feet, where she'd fallen in her haste to get away from Ray. She brushed a few leaves off Anna's sleeves. "Girl, you've got some taste in men."

Anna managed a laugh, then winced as a cut on her lip stung. She pressed it closed with trembling fingers. "Don't I know it. Is Mason okay?"

"He's just fine." Jake eased the baby over to her. "He calmed down almost as soon as I picked him up."

And Jake had just watched Chloe take down the drug-using kid. Just what every guy liked to see—a girl he liked involved in hand-to-hand combat. She pushed her hair back from her face, glancing down at her hand as she noticed stinging knuckles. Adrenaline must be fading. Just like Jake's admiration.

Bayley Conyers would have nothing less than hustling Anna and Mason straight into her car, a move Chloe felt fine about. Given Bayley's past dealing with a stalker, she'd have just the right touch with the young woman, who had to be battered body and soul.

Chloe and Jake followed. Alone again, the majority of the crowd across the parking lot on the lawn only marginally aware that anything had happened, Chloe shuffled backward toward her car. "I really need to be getting back to the house."

"Chloe." He reached for her fingertips, missed. "You were—"

"A control freak, too tough, taking over the situation, taking too many chances. I know." She turned to walk away.

His voice came from behind her, strong and steady. "I was going to say incredible. Exceptionally smart. Totally hot. Any of the above will work."

She stopped, her back going rigid. Was it possible that he really wouldn't prefer a more ladylike version of herself? Slowly, she pivoted to face him, not allowing anything to show on her face. "Don't joke."

"I'm not. You were awesome. You knew just how to get in that guy's head and defuse the situation without anyone getting hurt. I've never seen anything like it."

She took an uncertain step forward. "You were right there all along and had as much to do with it as I did."

"We work pretty well together." As she hesitated, Jake reached for her again, this time pulling her forward into his arms. He slid one hand into her silky hair, her soft vanilla scent wrapping around him as he released it.

"Don't you know how remarkable you are?" His eyes on hers, he leaned forward.

Her breath caught as his mouth hovered over hers, just a millisecond, really, but it seemed much longer. His lips brushed hers once, and again. She slid her hands up his chest to cup broad shoulders.

As he deepened the kiss, someone wolf-whistled and yelled, "Woohoo, go get 'em, Pastor Jake!"

She laughed against his mouth. "Love the privacy."

He waved at the crowd who had swiveled from watching the movie to watching them and gave a little bow, before pulling her around the corner of the building.

"You know what they're going to think." She arched an eyebrow.

"I couldn't care less what they think. We deserve a few minutes alone. I mean, seriously, we have four hundred chaperones right around the corner. How much trouble could we really be getting into?"

She laughed and held his hand as they walked toward a softly lit garden. He pulled her with him to sit on a small stone bench next to the centerpiece—a bubbling fountain of multicolored jars pouring water from one level to the next, the bubble and splash of the water echoing the rush of the ocean in the distance.

His legs stretched out, he sighed. "It's been a long day, don't you think?"

"So much has happened." And she'd had a weird feeling of being watched this afternoon. Maybe it was the hundreds of curious eyes wondering what she was doing with their pastor. Possibly just her imagination, but she still couldn't shake it. Chloe shivered.

"The nights are a little chilly yet. It'll stay that way until sometime in April or May, probably." His thumb circled over the sensitive skin of her palm. Inexplicably, tears clogged her throat.

Aftermath of the altercation with Anna's boyfriend, maybe. If she were a coward, she'd go with that. She wasn't.

She wouldn't be here in May. It wasn't fair to let him think she would be, even though he had to know that she'd be called to other cases eventually. "Jake, we need to talk about this."

"Let me go first, okay?" Jake rushed his words, maybe knowing, sensing somehow what she was going to say.

"Okay." With effort, she held her voice steady.

He looked around. "Did you know this garden was made for butterflies? It's really beautiful. You know... butterflies, they remind me of starting over with God, coming out of the cocoon into a new life."

He turned to her. "In a way, that's how I feel with you. That I've been given a second chance at love. You're an amazing woman, Chloe, and I have feelings for you. Deep, strong feelings for a strong, beautiful woman."

Once, barely balanced on a window ledge outside a window twenty stories up, Chloe had snapped photos that had put a mob crime boss away for life. At that moment, she'd felt equal measures of adrenaline and unadulterated fear. Those same emotions coursed through her now. She didn't want to make a wrong move, not with this precious man holding his heart out to her.

She hadn't meant to…but she'd fallen hard. Jake had a compassion for people unlike anything she'd ever seen. As deep as the evil was that she fought against, she saw that depth of goodness in Jake. He restored her hope in people.

She *wanted* to believe there could be something between the two of them.

Unfortunately it wasn't that simple. It took more than wishing and wanting. He was a hometown guy, one who had roots, and she didn't have anything close. She'd been undercover a long time, always on edge, always someone else. Some days she still had to think about who she was when she woke up in the morning.

But when she was with Jake, she felt like she knew.

He cleared his throat. "A guy could get a complex."

She smiled, a brief lift of the lips, but she didn't feel it, knew it didn't reach her eyes. "I'm not who you think I am, Jake. I may be strong enough to try and right the wrongs that criminals do, but I'm not strong enough to do this…to face the people of this town, this congregation every day."

He made a sound of protest, but she stopped him. She had to make him understand. "I'm not innocent. I've done things—*do* things, *see* things—in my job that they wouldn't understand. Most people can't handle it." With tears welling in her eyes, she told him the truth. "And I've been someone else for so long, I don't even know who I am."

Jake turned those startlingly blue eyes on her. They burned with an intensity that she couldn't name, but she wanted to fall into it and pray she never woke up. "*I* know who you are. You are God's. And you are mine."

He took her hands between his two big ones and rubbed them gently. "When you feel lost, I'll remind you."

It should make her feel nervous, or tweak her feminine outrage to hear him talk like that, but it didn't. It made her feel loved and wanted, and it was oh, so dangerous.

Jake's tender touch on her bruised knuckles where she'd taken down Anna's jerk boyfriend stung more than the wound. It scraped against those old desires she'd had as a kid. She so wanted to believe this could work out, but believing it would only bring more hurt when it didn't.

Jake gave his head a rueful shake. "I'm gonna sound like such a dork for saying this, but I didn't really fit in as a kid. You already know my mom was an alcoholic. It wasn't until my dad died and my grandmother took me in that I really understood what loving someone meant. She didn't love me because of who I was, she loved me in spite of it."

His voice cracked and he laughed a little. "It's so much easier to talk about this stuff from the pulpit."

She grinned. "Would it help if we went over there and I sat on the front row?"

He kissed her again, a quick, hard kiss. "No. I'm pretty sure I'd feel like a dork no matter where you were sitting."

"What does your grandmother have to do with me, Jake?"

"There's a passage in the Ephesians that says when we accept Him, we are adopted as His children. When I read that for the first time, it was like a light clicked on. God wants us to belong and loves us just like Gran loved me, except even more because He's not limited by humanity." He scrubbed a hand across his chin. "I know I'm messing this up."

She blinked and the tears she'd been fighting slid down her face. "No. You're not—I just don't know if I can believe it."

Jake looked straight into her deep brown eyes. "You can. God won't let you down, Chloe, no matter how often other people do." The pastor in him wanted her to know the truth, no matter how dorky it made him feel. The man in him wanted to pull her into his arms again and never let her go. "It caught me by surprise, you know."

"What?"

"You. Falling for you." He settled for pulling her close, snugging her against his side. In the churchyard, he could hear applause as *The Princess Bride* ended, Buttercup got rescued from a loveless life with Prince Humperdink and started her happily ever after with Westley.

Chloe was quiet, too quiet. He knew she had feelings for him. But would she be able to put those doubts from the past far enough behind her to trust him?

She drew in a shaky breath. "I think you care about me, Jake."

"Okay…" She wasn't giving him any big sigh of relief here. His heart began to feel like a wrestler was putting the squeeze on it.

She eased away from him on the bench and the ache intensified. "I'm leaving in the morning, Jake. There's a case in Austin, Texas. My team's already there."

He didn't say anything. He'd known he would be saying goodbye at some point, but he'd hoped…he'd prayed she'd be coming back.

Chloe touched his face, stroking his features almost as if she were memorizing them. "You deserve better. Someone who can truly be your partner here."

Pain had piled upon hurt this week, and this felt a lot like a knockout blow. Jake reeled as he took in her words. He wanted to hold on to her and not let her go, but he knew that would only push her away.

The only thing he could do was give her what she needed most. Understanding. "I love you, Chloe. I love the person you are right now and the person you will be in the future. I'll be here waiting for you when you finish your case and want to come home."

Her eyes filled again, but she opened them wide, refusing to let the tears come. Stubborn woman.

Leaning forward, she smoothed one small hand

across his cheek, placing a soft kiss on the other one. Jake closed his eyes. When he opened them, she was walking away.

Home. It was a word that Chloe had never really believed in. But as she let herself into Bayley's brightly colored beach house, she could almost feel it. She'd bounced between houses all her life, keeping her battered backpack under her bed at each place. Foster kids, which was what she was regardless of the fact that she was mostly with relatives, never knew when they'd be moving on a moment's notice.

Things changed. At least, that's what the case workers always said.

Come to think of it, that lifestyle wasn't too different from what she was living now. She always had her go-bag. Ready for the call-out. It was her choice, her terms now. But it was still the same nomad life. Moving to new places on a moment's notice. Only her sugar-cookie candles were the same from place to place.

It was funny, though, now that she'd had the real thing, those candles didn't seem to do it for her anymore. She'd felt a sense of belonging in tiny, charming Sea Breeze, Florida. Maybe she'd been craving that home-baked-cookie sense of home more than she'd realized.

She flipped a couple of lights on and kicked off her shoes. More than that coming-home feeling, she'd found something even more unexpected. A sense of peace that she'd never experienced, along with a troublesome sense that there was more for her in life than she ever imagined.

Jake might've thought he was bungling his personal message tonight, but it was everything she needed to hear. Every word had soaked into dry soil, watering seeds that had been planted years ago but shriveled with no care. Now those same seeds seemed to be springing to life, prompting her to seek more.

She just wasn't sure that *more* included Jake.

Not that she didn't want it to…she was flat-out in love with him. But she'd meant what she'd said. He deserved more than she could offer him.

A knock at the door startled her. Oh, Jake. If she'd learned anything along the way, it was that a longer goodbye didn't make it hurt any less.

Chloe reached for the doorknob, pulling the door open. Halfway there, she stopped, surprised. "Well, you're not who I was expecting. Come on in."

She turned to close the door and heard her visitor closing the shades on the large picture windows. "Probably not a bad idea. I always forget to pull them at night."

Before she could turn around, she heard the unmistakable sound of a round being chambered in a semi-automatic.

Jake said good-night to the church crowd as they left the movie, accepting some good-natured ribbing for the kiss he'd shared with Chloe in full view of the watching congregation. In hindsight that hadn't been his smartest move ever, but admittedly he hadn't exactly been thinking about the ramifications at the time.

He walked to his truck and beeped the locks open. His fingers on the door handle, he stopped. He didn't want to go home to his empty condo, alone. Wanting someone to go through life with wasn't something new for him, but finding Chloe and not being able to be with her…that was a new level of loneliness that he really didn't want to explore. Not tonight.

He knew going into that conversation with Chloe that it might not go the way he wanted it to. He wasn't sure exactly what he'd expected. She was afraid to trust—she'd been let down so many times. So he'd just have to prove to her that he was different and meant what he said. Again and again until she believed that he wasn't like them—the rest of the people in her life who'd let her down.

He stopped in his office door and looked at his desk in disgust. It was stacked with stuff he never seemed to get to on a regular day, and this week had been even worse. Before he could start on that pile, though, he had one more thing he needed to do. He'd started a letter to the congregation about the fire and what to expect in the next six months, but he'd sent the first draft to Susan to proof. If she'd had a chance to look at it, maybe he could finish it up and get it ready for the volunteers to mail tomorrow.

At Susan's desk, he jiggled the mouse, bringing her computer to life. The problem was finding the letter. He went to click on My Documents, missed, and ended up clicking Pictures instead. She had about fifty picture folders on this computer, each labeled by date, some as recent as this week.

He knew Susan kept files of church pictures for the Web site, but what did she have from this week? Pictures of the cleanup? He hadn't seen her there with the camera. He opened the file and as each picture in the gallery came into focus, shock slammed him.

These weren't church photos. These were photos Susan had taken of him at the coffee shop, photos of him with Chloe. Photos of Chloe alone on the deck at Bayley's house and Chloe working at the fire inspector's office. He clicked open the next file.

Photos popped up of him with baby Mason on the church playground while Anna went to get her driver's license renewed. Anna moving into her tiny apartment, and Anna and Mason in the nursery at the church, shot through the window of the nursery. A sense of horrified realization began to creep in on him.

Susan had been stalking them all.

But what about Sharon Hardin?

He picked a date before Sharon's death and found photos of him having coffee with Sharon on the porch of Sailor's shop. And him holding the door open for Sharon to get into her car on the day she was killed.

He grabbed the phone, tried Chloe's number. It went straight to voice mail. He punched in Gabe's number. No answer.

He looked at the files again. The earliest file wasn't a date. It had a name. *Eva.*

The cursor hesitated over the folder. He took a deep breath and double-clicked. Pictures flooded the page. Hundreds of them. Wedding pictures of Susan with her husband? And later, baby pictures. The couple standing in front of a sold sign with the baby…their first house? *Oh, dear God, no.*

He recognized that house.

It had been his first six months as a firefighter. That call-out had been his first house fire where there were fatalities. He'd been the one to find the baby. The fire hadn't reached her room, but the smoke…the smoke was so thick. They would never have found her if they hadn't had the thermal-imaging camera. The EMTs worked on the baby for twenty minutes, but they couldn't revive her.

The dad had been taken to the hospital, but he never woke up.

Jake had felt so guilty about losing them—his first. And he'd been the rookie, the most inexperienced on the crew. Had he hesitated, had he taken a wrong turn that could have cost them precious seconds? He'd agonized over every step, but in the end, the captain had convinced him that they'd done everything they could in the time they had.

Sometimes even when you did everything right, the fire still won.

If his memory was accurate, the mom had been out of town on a business trip. He clicked on a newspaper article. She'd been in New York at market buying for the children's shop she was scheduled to open the next month. She'd bought the baby a christening gown. And instead of being baptized in it, the baby girl had been buried in it. But that woman's name wasn't Susan Paulson, it was Marissa.

He dialed Gabe's number again, looking closer at the picture in the file. Blond hair and brown eyes. But… something about the face. He zoomed in. If you colored the hair brown and added blue contacts, it would be Susan.

He'd met her at the funeral. Told her how very sorry he was that they hadn't gotten there in time. Was that why she'd chosen him?

No answer from Gabe. He dialed Chloe's number again. Again he got voice mail. Either she'd turned her phone off because she didn't want to talk to him, or she was in trouble. Would her guard be down because they all thought Elaine was in custody?

No. Chloe didn't completely buy that Elaine was the killer in the first place. She wouldn't let her guard down. She was fine.

Still, he dialed her number again as he clicked on today's file folder. Jake kissing Chloe with the whole church looking on. The two of them in the butterfly garden. The thought of someone watching them, taking advantage of such a vulnerable moment made him want to throw up.

At that instant, he remembered the photos that had come to his desk. In every photo, Chloe's face had been the one X'd out.

His heart thundered in his chest as he knew with certainty. Chloe wasn't fine.

She was the target.

His phone rang. Thank God. "Chloe?"

Instead of Chloe's voice, he heard a deep laugh. "You're so sad. It's Gabe. I got your friend Ray settled in jail and just wanted to check and see if you had Anna taken care of."

"She's at Bayley's. Gabe, Elaine is not the killer." His breath came in jerks as he sprinted for his truck, not bothering to lock the doors or set the alarm.

"We've been through this, Jake. Elaine confessed."

Jake started the truck with a roar and slammed it into Reverse. "There's something you need to see at the church, Gabe, on Susan's computer. Except I'm pretty sure her name isn't Susan Paulson. It's Marissa McAllister."

"Are you sure about this?" Gabe didn't sound sure, not anymore.

"You weren't here then, but a few years ago when I was a rookie firefighter, Marissa's husband and baby died in a fire. I found pictures on her computer. Hundreds of them, Gabe. The person in those pictures is definitely Susan."

Gabe was quiet.

"She's the one who sent me the pictures of Chloe with the face X'd out. She's the one who brought the drugged cookies. When I think how easy I made it for her… Gabe, I can't get in touch with Chloe."

Gabe murmured something to someone at his location and then came back on the line. "You think that Susan is the one who killed Julie and Sharon."

"It makes sense. And if she wants to get to me by killing people who are close to me, she's going after Chloe. She has the motive, something Elaine never had."

"I just sent someone to Susan's address and to Chloe's. We'll get her, don't worry." Gabe murmured something that Jake couldn't hear to others in the room.

Jake turned onto Shellfish Drive, his tires skidding in the loose oyster shells that paved the street. Chloe's house was at the end, but he could see smoke beginning to seep from the cracks at the roofline. "You better call out the fire trucks. The house is on fire. Chloe's in there."

"Jake, beach police are on their way. I'll scramble the fire department and they'll be there in minutes. *Do not go in.*" Gabe's voice level rose as he admonished Jake.

"Chloe may not have minutes." He slammed the truck into Park in a driveway two houses down and pulled his gear from the back.

"And you don't have the right equipment." Gabe was directing people in his department in between yelling at Jake. "Promise me, Jake."

"I can't." He flipped his phone closed and stuffed it in one of the pockets of his turnout coat. It wasn't going to help where he was going, but he might need it later. *Hang on, Chloe. Hang on, baby. I'm coming to get you.*

THIRTEEN

Chloe heard popping and crackling. The kind of sound that a roaring fire in the fireplace made. She loved that sound on a cold winter day…. Somewhere in the back of her mind, a memory tickled. It wasn't a good sound. *Come on, Chloe. Wake up.*

Wake up, wake up, wake up. Open your eyes.

Why was she so sleepy? What happened last night? She remembered coming home after a conversation with Jake. Someone knocked on the door and she opened it, but it wasn't Jake. It was his assistant, Susan. Susan whom nobody suspected because she supported Jake one hundred percent, who had been around since before Julie's murder. Susan, who wore high heels and baked cookies with drugs in them to make Jake more susceptible to her suggestions.

Drugs. Had she been drugged? She'd heard the blinds being pulled closed and she'd started to turn around when she'd heard the round being chambered.

She'd faced Susan then and tried to talk to her, wishing

all the while that she hadn't locked up her service weapon before she'd left for the picnic this afternoon.

"You don't want to do that, Susan."

Susan smiled, but it wasn't a smile, it was a brittle curve that looked like it might shatter at any second. "Oh, you have no idea how much I want to do this."

"Why?"

Susan pulled a piece of paper out of the pocket of her jeans. A photograph.

"Your family?"

"The baby's name was Eva." Susan held the picture out to Chloe.

"And your husband?"

"He died in the hospital, but it was all their fault."

Jake's fault? Was that what this had been about? "Whose fault, Susan? But that's not your real name, is it?"

The gun wavered, but remained steady.

"I haven't been Marissa in a long, long time." She took the picture back and stared at it. "The firefighters came, but they didn't save them. They pulled my baby girl out, not a scratch on her, not a burn."

There was the motive. "There was a whole squad there. Why did you choose Jake?"

"He was the weak link. He came to the funeral with his blue eyes all watery." The contempt in Susan's voice turned Chloe's stomach. "He even apologized. But what he didn't tell me was that he was the rookie. If he hadn't been there slowing them down, my family would still be alive."

Her logic was totally irrational, but Susan's mind had been warped by the grief and loss. She'd convinced herself that Jake was to blame. And all of this…retribution…had been to make him pay for her loss.

What a waste.

"I understand, Susan. I understand why you want him to pay." She coughed.

Susan's eyes burned with anger. "You can't possibly understand what I lost."

Actually, Chloe thought she could. She'd lost a family herself. A mom and a dad who'd loved her. And later, she'd lost again. And again. It hadn't been anyone's fault. But she'd been blaming them anyway. Blaming God.

Chloe coughed, deeper. Why couldn't she seem to catch her breath? *It wasn't anyone's fault. It just was. And the victory came from the way she handled it. The way she learned to love.*

She'd been trying to keep herself independent to keep from losing love again. How ridiculous. As if she'd stop loving Jake just because she wouldn't be with him.

A knife blade of pain seared through her shoulder.

Susan shot her.

That's why she'd blacked out. Susan had shot her just as she'd realized the truth—she'd almost thrown away the best thing to ever happen to her.

She wouldn't stop loving Jake, no matter where she was in the world. Jake.

Jake. She snapped open her eyes. And pain slammed into her head.

She groaned, putting her hand to her head. Drugs. She hadn't been shot with a bullet. She'd been shot with a tranquilizer. Pushing back the nausea, she tried to draw in a deep breath, but coughed instead, shards of pain shooting through her head.

She forced her eyes to open again. *Oh, please, God, help.* Smoke filled the room, seeping under the closed door and shooting toward the ceiling, swirling in circles. It was coming for her.

Jake buckled his coat and pulled up the collar, stopping only to wet a bandanna at Mrs. P.'s hose and tie it around his face. Every second felt like an eternity, knowing that Chloe was up there possibly fighting for her life. But he knew firsthand that the gear might be the one thing that could get him and Chloe out alive. He slammed his helmet on his head.

Not knowing what he would find, he ran for the house, his only weapon a fire extinguisher he grabbed from under the seat of the truck at the last minute. Every breath was a prayer that Chloe was still alive. Susan had panicked with Anna when time was short and Anna had survived. Did she change her pattern to make sure of the outcome or did she stick to her profile?

There was no way to predict.

Jake took the stairs to the house two at a time. He paused at the top, took as deep a breath as possible and kicked the door in. Black smoke billowed out into his face, vicious heat right behind it. Flashes, memories, of another fire scene bombarded him. The panic thick in his blood, flames licking at his boots, climbing the walls, as he'd tried to reach his best friend.

But this wasn't Julie's house. This fire wouldn't end

the same way. Because he'd known to look for Chloe. And Chloe was still alive. *Please, God, let her be alive.*

He knew she wouldn't be in the front room, but without a crew of people coming behind him, he had to check. Placing the fire extinguisher on the table, he cleared the room as quickly as possible, the acrid air growing thicker and more impossible to see through. He dropped to his knees as his eyes poured tears.

Opening the bedroom door, he tried to yell for her and ended up in a coughing fit instead. Like the other crime scenes, this one had been set. And now that he knew, he could see it was a nursery. The tiny figurine, the silver cross.

The bed was empty. Where was she?

He lifted the dust ruffle on the bed. Chloe had crawled as far under as she could. The air here was the clearest in the house. She'd done good.

"Chloe." His voice rasped out louder. "Chloe."

She didn't move. *Oh, dear God, was he too late?*

He touched her bare foot. She didn't pull it away, but it was warm. Something crashed to the floor in the big front room. They were running out of time.

Pulling her out from under the bed, he felt for the pulse at the base of her neck. He couldn't tell. He couldn't tell if he was feeling his pounding heart or hers.

Jake unsnapped the buckles of his coat and slid out of it. He lifted Chloe and wrapped it around her. The sounds of the fire told him he had seconds to get out. Gripping Chloe in his arms, he stood. Searing pain shot from his thigh up his back. He blocked it out. It didn't matter. Nothing mattered but getting Chloe out. He would die before he would let anything happen to her.

In the great room, the fire raged, greedy. Circling, diving, sucking every bit of life from the air.

He rushed for the door. Fresh air. Freedom from this inferno. He could almost taste it.

A roar came from the dark corner of the great room. Susan streaked across the room and tackled Jake from behind. He braced himself for the impact, protecting Chloe as much as possible. His legs gave way. Burning embers seared into his skin as he hit the floor, but he pushed it out of his mind.

Chloe. He shoved her closer to the front door where the firefighters would see her first in his reflective gear.

He kicked up, trying to get Susan off of him. Futile. The injury limited his motion and Susan had rage and planning on her side. She slammed him into the floor and he stared into the eyes of insanity.

"Susan, why are you doing this?" He managed to gasp out the words. He needed to hear it from her, the woman he'd trusted as a friend for the last three years.

Her fingers dug into the tender skin around his throat. "You let my baby die. You were the weak link."

The edges of Jake's vision began to gray. "It doesn't have to be this way."

The woman who killed in the name of her baby and husband only tightened her grip. "I wanted you to suffer like I've suffered, but I'll let you die in the flames like she did."

He caught a movement out of the corner of his eye.

Chloe picked up the fire extinguisher. She angled it toward the back of Susan's head, missed slightly. The tank grazed the back of Susan's head and slammed into her shoulder.

Susan slumped to the side. Jake didn't see her. All he could see was Chloe, swaying to the floor. He reached her in seconds, lifting her into his arms. Tears poured down his face. He didn't know if it was the smoke or because she was alive.

He was so grateful. He stumbled out the door onto the deck, which smoldered and burned, too. The fire trucks were on scene.

Matt Clark, running point, met him on the stairs. He pulled his mask back. "Can I take her?"

Jake shook his head, coughed. "Susan. Inside."

Matt didn't hesitate, but pulled his gear into place and with the rest of the squad behind him, headed into the flames.

Jake made it as far as Mrs. Phillips's yard. His back gave out, the pain a tearing force he couldn't fight against anymore. He put Chloe on her feet as gray swirled into his vision. He hit his knees.

"Jake?" He heard her raspy, smoke-damaged voice. Then nothing.

Jake opened his eyes. The pain in his back, while still searing, had eased enough for him to take a shaky breath. He struggled to sit up, but half a dozen hands pushed him down on the rigid backboard, one holding a mask over his face. He shoved it away.

"Chloe?"

"I'm right here, Jake." She coughed as she held her own oxygen mask away from her mouth to speak.

The sea of firefighters parted, giving her room beside him. She brought a blanket with her, shudders still racking her body. Aftermath of the close call, probably. If she'd been dealing with major burns, they'd have already LifeFlighted her out of here.

He noticed that he and Chloe were the center of attention of the circle of faces around them, all his friends. "Do you mind?"

Matt Clark grinned, a slash of white in a grimy face. "Yeah, we do, but don't worry, bro. We won't tease you. Much."

Putting them out of his mind, Jake looked up into Chloe's worried brown eyes as the EMT started an IV in his arm. "Hey, no worries, Chloe. I'm tough."

He coughed, and the tears started to slide down her face, leaving tracks in the sooty residue.

"I'm so sorry," she rasped.

"Don't be. I understand." He cupped her cheek with one rough, bleeding hand. "Chloe, I love you. I'm not letting you go. But, baby, you don't have to be a pastor's wife. If you want to live in Virginia, I'll move there and be an FBI agent's husband. I just don't want to live my life without you in it."

Chloe's heart seemed to stutter to a stop. She loved this man so much. She'd already made her decision before he offered to give up his life here, but the fact that he did…how could she do any less?

Once again, he'd laid his heart out there for her. His expression was somewhere between desperate hope and maybe the fear that she wouldn't be strong enough to hold on to what they had. But he didn't know her well enough to know how stubborn she was…yet.

Her lips trembled as she tried to smile. "I don't care where we live. I just don't want to lose you."

She watched as comprehension sank in and his eyes filled. "Oh, Jake."

He didn't speak, but the hand on her cheek caressed gently. She reached for it with both of hers. "I love you, Jake Rollins."

"Are you ready for this, Chloe, really ready?" His voice rasped as he asked.

"I've taken a lot of chances, but I was afraid to risk my heart. Afraid to love you, thinking somehow I'd protect myself from being hurt." She knew now that she'd walked the edge with Jake, and been so afraid of falling. Now she was ready to risk everything she had, everything for the chance to love him. Simply put, she knew he'd catch her.

"Loving's not easy." He coughed and one of the paramedics pushed the oxygen mask back over his face.

"It'll be worth it for you."

Jake pushed the mask away again. "Sorry, bud. There's something I need to do."

He reached for Chloe, pulling her close. "I love you." His arms closed around her and when he kissed her, she knew that it didn't matter where she lived. Wherever Jake was, that was home.

Jake whispered in Chloe's ear. "Will you be my wife?"

The answer seemed so obvious to her now. And now that she understood what was really important, she could see how seamlessly their lives could blend together.

She nodded, her lips touching his once more.

The firefighters surrounding them whooped and cheered. Matt Clark high-fived someone across their heads. Lara Hughes applauded, her eyes full.

EMT Daniel Hudson rolled the gurney close and, with his partner's help, lowered it to the ground. "Jake, my friend, I'm sorry to tell you, you've won yourself an all-inclusive trip to the trauma unit."

Chloe tried to move away, but Jake gripped her hand tighter. "I'll be fine, Chloe."

"Hang on, here we go." With a nod, the EMTs lifted him in unison. His mouth grew tight, and what color he'd had in his cheeks drained.

He'd come for her. He'd saved her life, and it had cost him so much.

Lara helped Chloe stand and draped the blanket around her shoulders. Her heart in her throat, she watched as they rolled Jake away.

"Come on, I'll help you." Lara picked up the portable oxygen and looked at Chloe, a quizzical look in her pretty hazel eyes. "Well, you are going with him, right?"

Chloe tried to laugh and ended up coughing instead. "Just try and stop me."

Chloe brushed Jake's hair away from his forehead. He was resting, but there were lines around his mouth that hadn't been there yesterday.

He roused, long black eyelashes lifting to reveal gorgeous sea-blue eyes that warmed when they saw her. And then turned questioning when they saw her strange attire.

She'd thrown on an FBI jacket over scrubs to go down to the police station to check on Elaine Barbury and Susan—Marissa McAllister.

"You've been to work?" He held his hand out. The trust implied in the gesture answered a question she didn't know she'd been asking.

She released a long, deep breath. "I went to talk to Elaine and check on Susan."

"And?"

"Elaine admitted she gave a false confession. She's definitely got a history of acting out in revenge, but she's not twisted, just confused. And she's not an arsonist, she blows things up." Realizing how ridiculous that sounded, she rolled her eyes and laughed.

She continued. "I'm no psychiatrist, but I'm pretty sure her acting out stems back to being abandoned by her father. She felt dismissed by Randy when he didn't want a relationship after a couple of dates. Then, when he wouldn't let her on the range with her prize gun, it struck at the heart of her insecurity. So, she took retribution."

She poured water into a cup for Jake. "Thirsty?"

"Thanks. I knew that Elaine had some issues, but had no idea it was that bad." He shifted on the mattress, his face pulling in pain.

Her heart squeezed. "Once I dug a little deeper into her discharge from the army, I found that's the same problem she had there. Some guy doesn't pick her for the unit softball team and suddenly his car is blowing up. Turns out that's actually how she got in the army in the first place. One of her teachers refused to give her a grade she needed to graduate, so she vandalized the teacher's car. As an alternative to doing time, the judge gave her the option of getting her G.E.D. and joining the army, hopefully to straighten her out. Instead, she learned to blow things up."

"And maybe if she'd gotten help, none of this would've happened." He squeezed her hand. "Susan?"

Chloe sighed. "They've got her on suicide watch. The department psychologist thinks she latched on to revenge as her reason to live after her family died. Without that, she might try to kill herself." She hesitated. "Jake, it could've been anyone. It just happened to be you."

"I know." His eyes were dark with pain and something else. Regret?

"Nobody saw it in her, Jake. Dr. VanDoren thinks that killing Julie made Susan feel powerful. The other, smaller fires were set to stem the urge to kill again. The recent murders were an effort to reclaim the power she felt the first time as she got more and more out of control emotionally. That's why they got closer and less organized. Because killing someone else really didn't solve her problems."

Jake held Chloe's hand, reassuring himself that she really was here, sitting beside him. Despite the pain that

Susan had caused him, he could be grateful that he had this incredible woman in his life. "I'm unbelievably lucky."

She raised her eyebrows in question.

He gave her a searching look. "I know in the aftermath of adrenaline, you know, the flash of the moment, sometimes people say things they regret later."

"What exactly are you talking about, Jake?"

In a rush, the words spilled out. "You told me you loved me."

"And I don't want to take it back." She laughed, probably at the pained expression on his face that had nothing to do with his back.

"I don't want to push you. So you can if you want."

She leaned forward, capturing his mouth in a kiss, making him laugh.

He looked into her eyes, dark brown velvet. "This is *so* not the way I imagined this."

"What?" Her look was perplexed.

From under the sheet, he pulled out the small, black velvet box that he'd sent Matt Clark on a supersecret mission to find. He heard her gasp and smiled.

"When did you… How did you…" He opened the box. "Oh, *Jake.*"

"It was my grandmother's. I know it's old-fashioned, so if you want something different—"

"It's absolutely perfect." Her fingers shook as she held her hand out.

He held her hand in both of his. "You know being a preacher's wife isn't always a fairy tale."

"Psh. I've played a lot of roles in my life. How hard could being a pastor's wife be?"

As he slid the engagement ring into place, Chloe knew it was right. No more doubts. She looked forward into a bright future because after all she and Jake had been through, she knew that however tough the challenges they faced, they could meet them together.

EPILOGUE

For about the twentieth time already today, Jake wished that he didn't have to use the stupid cane. But he was on his feet, walking, a blessing from God and good rehab.

He wanted to stand at the altar of the church when his bride walked down the aisle. She'd chosen simple guitar music, but even so, as the chords changed, his heart picked up the pace. The doors at the back of the church opened and there she was.

Jake caught his breath. She had flowers in her hair and a simple, breezy white dress that came down to her ankles. She was beautiful. She was barefoot.

He laughed. She was already doing things her way.

Everyone had always told him he wouldn't remember his own wedding. He'd laughed at them, not believing that he'd ever forget the day that he'd waited so long for. But it passed in a blur of the congregation standing and applauding, tasting the cake, and many, many congratulations.

Finally, the wedding coordinator whisked them toward the door. As she stood waiting for the doors to open, Chloe pulled a tiny slip of paper out of her bouquet. "The time is right to make new friends."

"I didn't know you were sentimental, Chloe."

"I'm not." She laughed out loud as she waved a couple of middle school boys from the youth group forward with huge baskets of favors for their guests…baskets full of fortune cookies.

She stood on her tiptoes and whispered in his ear. "I love you. Are you ready to start our new life?"

He looked into her eyes, shining with emotion today. "Yes, I am. But only with you—I love you, too."

She pushed open the doors and pulled him through them, a wide smile on her face. He stalled out.

The entire police force had gathered, backed by his brothers from the fire department. In their dress blues, they formed a corridor. As Chloe stopped at the top of the stairs and drew him forward, Cruse Conyers hollered something indecipherable and twenty swords formed an archway.

Jake leaned over to whisper in Chloe's ear. "What's all this?"

She gave him an impudent look. "It's customary for the police department to turn out when one of their own gets married."

He grabbed Chloe by the waist, sweeping her off her feet. "You got the job?"

She laughed, wrapping her arms around his neck as she slid back to her bare feet with their baby-pink toenail polish. "I got the job."

He looked down at Chloe, his *wife*. Would he ever get

tired of saying that? "Well, Lieutenant *Rollins*. I guess that means you're going to be sticking around Sea Breeze. Putting down roots."

"Yeah, I guess it does." She grinned and grabbed him by the hand, starting down the aisle between her new brothers-at-arms, who cheered them into a new life. Together.

* * * * *

Dear Reader,

Some people have extremely dangerous jobs. These unique men and women make life-and-death decisions every day. In their ordinary work life, they are called upon to do extraordinary things. These are the people who inspired the EMERALD COAST 911 series.

But is being a hero only about what you do, or is it also about who you are? In *Smoke Screen,* when Jake could no longer be a firefighter, he had to dig deep to find that God had a stronger calling for him. And he had to learn that it wasn't the dramatic rescue that made him a hero in Chloe's eyes, it was the fact that he was there for her when she needed him, every time.

Thanks so much for picking up Jake and Chloe's story. For more information on my books, please visit www.stephanienewtonbooks.com or e-mail me at newtonwriter@gmail.com.

All the best,

Stephanie Newton

QUESTIONS FOR DISCUSSION

1. Jake Rollins's life changed when he was injured. He accepts that God has a new calling for him, but he misses his life as a firefighter. Have you ever experienced a life change that totally altered things for you?

2. Chloe Davis has spent a lot of time undercover. She's used to operating on her own. How does that change when she gets to Sea Breeze?

3. How does Jake feel about bringing danger to the people of Sea Breeze? Could he have done anything to stop it?

4. Chloe believes in God, but she has a harder time believing that she can find God in church. What led her to believe that and how does Jake's church make her feel welcome?

5. From the beginning Chloe is intrigued by Jake. What is different about him that makes him appealing to her? Why?

6. Chloe uses the candles to make her impersonal hotel rooms feel like a home. How does she realize what she's been missing?

7. What makes a hero? Is it someone willing to walk into a burning building? Or can ordinary people be heroes, too?

8. Jake's grandmother was a central figure in his life. She taught him to manage his pain and fear, to trust God and to serve others. Who are the teachers in your life? What are you learning?

9. Jake has really good friends in Sea Breeze, something Chloe realizes that she's missing. Can you name some of their friends and how they show their friendship for Chloe and Jake?

10. Both Susan and Elaine had real problems. Do you think that anything could have diverted them from the path that they took?

11. Sometimes life doesn't turn out the way we think it's going to. What did Jake and Chloe have to say goodbye to, and how did God show Jake and Chloe He had a new plan for them?

12. Jake risks his ability to walk to save Chloe from the fire. What gives him the strength to do that?

13. Chloe feels strong and brave with her badge and gun, but she can't hide behind it with Jake. She has to risk everything to love him. Why does she decide to take a chance with Jake?

*Scandal surrounds Rebecca Gunderson after
she shares a storm cellar during a deadly
tornado with Pete Benjamin.
No one believes the time she spent with
him was totally innocent.
Can Pete protect her reputation?*

*Read on for a sneak peek of
HEARTLAND WEDDING by Renee Ryan
Book 2 in the AFTER THE STORM:
THE FOUNDING YEARS series
available February 2010
from Love Inspired Historical.*

"Marry me," Pete demanded, realizing his mistake as the words left his mouth. He hadn't asked her. He'd told her.

He tried to rectify his insensitive act but Rebecca was already speaking over him. "Why are you willing to spend the rest of your life married to a woman you hardly know?"

"Because it's the right thing to do," he said.

Angling her head, she caught her bottom lip between her teeth and then did something utterly remarkable. She smoothed her fingertips across his forehead. "As sweet as I think your gesture is, you don't have to save me."

A pleasant warmth settled over him at her touch, leaving him oddly disoriented. "Yes, I do."

She dropped her hand to her side. "I don't mind what others say about me. You and I, *we* know the truth."

Pete caught her hand in his, and turned it over in his palm. "I told Matilda Johnson we were getting married."

She snatched her hand free. "You…you…*what?*"

He spoke more slowly this time. "I told her we were getting married."

She did *not* like his answer. That much was made clear by her scowl. "You shouldn't have done that."

"She was blaming you for luring me into my own storm cellar."

The color leached out of Rebecca's cheeks as she sank into a nearby chair. "I…I simply don't know what to say."

"Say yes. Mrs. Johnson is a bully. Our marriage will silence her. I'll speak with the pastor today and—"

"No."

"—schedule the ceremony at once." His words came to a halt. "What did you say?"

"I said, no." She rose cautiously, her palms flat on her thighs as though to brace herself. "I won't marry you."

"You're turning me down? After everything that's happened today?"

"No. I mean, *yes.* I'm turning you down."

"Your reputation—"

"Is my concern, not yours."

She sniffed, rather loudly, but she didn't give in to her emotions. Oh, she blinked. And blinked. And *blinked.* But no tears spilled from her eyes.

Pete pulled in a hard breath. He'd never been more baffled by a woman. "We were both in my storm cellar," he reminded her through a painfully tight jaw. "That means we share the burden of the consequences equally."

Blink, blink, blink. "My decision is final."

"So is mine. We'll be married by the end of the day."

Her breathing quickened to short, hard pants. And then...*at last*...it happened. One lone tear slipped from her eye.

"Rebecca, please," he whispered, knowing his soft manner came too late.

"No." She wrapped her dignity around her like a coat of ironclad armor. "We have nothing more to say to each other."

Just as another tear plopped onto the toe of her shoe, she turned and rushed out of the kitchen.

Stunned, Pete stared at the empty space she'd occupied. "That," he said to himself, "could have gone better."

Will Pete be able to change Rebecca's mind
and salvage her reputation?
Find out in HEARTLAND WEDDING
available in February 2010
only from Love Inspired Historical.

Love Inspired.
HISTORICAL
INSPIRATIONAL HISTORICAL ROMANCE

After taking shelter from a deadly tornado, Rebecca Gundersen finds herself at the center of a new storm—gossip. She says the time she spent in the storm cellar with Pete Benjamin was totally innocent, but no one believes her. Marriage is the only way to save her reputation....

AFTER *the* **STORM**
The Founding Years

Look for
Heartland Wedding
by
RENEE RYAN

Steeple
Hill®

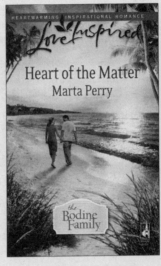

LARGER-PRINT BOOKS!

GET 2 FREE
LARGER-PRINT NOVELS
PLUS 2 FREE
MYSTERY GIFTS

Love Inspired®
SUSPENSE
RIVETING INSPIRATIONAL ROMANCE

Larger-print novels are now available...

YES! Please send me 2 FREE LARGER-PRINT Love Inspired® Suspense novels and my 2 FREE mystery gifts (gifts are worth about $10). After receiving them, if I don't wish to receive any more books, I can return the shipping statement marked "cancel". If I don't cancel, I will receive 4 brand-new novels every month and be billed just $4.74 per book in the U.S. or $5.24 per book in Canada. That's a saving of over 20% off the cover price. It's quite a bargain! Shipping and handling is just 50¢ per book in the U.S. and 75¢ per book in Canada.* I understand that accepting the 2 free books and gifts places me under no obligation to buy anything. I can always return a shipment and cancel at any time. Even if I never buy another book, the two free books and gifts are mine to keep forever.

110 IDN E4AN 310 IDN E4AY

Name _____ (PLEASE PRINT) _____

Address _____ Apt. # _____

City _____ State/Prov. _____ Zip/Postal Code _____

Signature (if under 18, a parent or guardian must sign)

Mail to **Steeple Hill Reader Service:**
IN U.S.A.: P.O. Box 1867, Buffalo, NY 14240-1867
IN CANADA: P.O. Box 609, Fort Erie, Ontario L2A 5X3

Not valid for current subscribers to Love Inspired Suspense larger-print books.

**Are you a current subscriber to Love Inspired Suspense books and want to receive the larger-print edition?
Call 1-800-873-8635 or visit www.morefreebooks.com.**

* Terms and prices subject to change without notice. Prices do not include applicable taxes. Sales tax applicable in N.Y. Canadian residents will be charged applicable provincial taxes and GST. Offer not valid in Quebec. This offer is limited to one order per household. All orders subject to approval. Credit or debit balances in a customer's account(s) may be offset by any other outstanding balance owed by or to the customer. Please allow 4 to 6 weeks for delivery. Offer available while quantities last.

Your Privacy: Steeple Hill Books is committed to protecting your privacy. Our Privacy Policy is available online at www.SteepleHill.com or upon request from the Reader Service. From time to time we make our lists of customers available to reputable third parties who have a product or service of interest to you. If you would prefer we not share your name and address, please check here. ☐

Help us get it right—We strive for accurate, respectful and relevant communications. To clarify or modify your communication preferences, visit us at www.ReaderService.com/consumerchoice.

LISUSLP10